Keeping Eileen

CHRIS KENISTON
USA TODAY BESTSELLING AUTHOR

Indie House Publishing

Indie House Publishing

BOOKS BY CHRIS KENISTON

Head Over Heels
Perfect Match
Just One Kiss
It Had to Be You

OTHER BOOKS BY CHRIS KENISTON

Honeymoon Series
Honeymoon for One
Honeymoon for Three

Family Secrets Novels
Champagne Sisterhood
The Homecoming
Hope's Corner

Original Aloha Series
Waikiki Wedding

ACKNOWLEDGEMENTS

Writing *Keeping Eileen* has been a true writer's journey. This book had me pulling out my hair on some days and delightedly tapping at the keyboard on others. I can only hope everyone gets as much pleasure from the finished project as I have.

Along the way, during those massive hair pulling escapades, my dear friends, authors Kathy Ivan and Linda Steinberg came to my rescue— more than once. For consuming way more Chinese food than we should while rehashing and brainstorming this story, I owe them a tremendous debt of gratitude!

I'd be remiss in my duties as former college classmate and friend if I didn't thank my maid of honor Diane Borgia and her ever patient husband Jim for allowing me to invade their peaceful, quiet home for weeks at a time to get Eileen's story written.

Thanks always go to my family. A supportive and loving little clan of my own who get it when Mom says, "Not now, I'm writing." Love you all.

And to every last one of my fans who has enjoyed this journey with me and the Farradays—thank you! Thank you for reading, for sticking with me, for sending me notes, for writing reviews, for telling your friends, for just being you!

CHAPTER ONE

"**O**f all the gin joints in all the world." Eileen Callahan, known as Aunt Eileen to half the town, swallowed hard and blinked. When two more steps left Glenn Baker towering over her table, she squeezed her eyes tightly shut and grabbed onto the edge of the table. Slowly opening her eyes, the vision was still standing in front of her, sporting a shaky smile.

"Hello," he croaked out.

"Why, Mr. Baker," Meg Farraday, Eileen's niece-in-law, pushed to her feet. "What a pleasant surprise. Glad you decided to venture out of your room."

His gaze locked on Eileen. "Decided I was hungry after all. There was no one at the cafe." He shifted his attention to Meg. "Followed the music here."

"Then you are in luck because O'Fearadaigh's has the best corned beef and cabbage this side of the Blarney Stone."

"Does it now?" His gaze once again shifted to Eileen. "It's nice to see you, Leeni."

If for even a moment Eileen had considered her mind was playing tricks on her, the use of the nickname that only Glenn called her removed all doubt–this man was no hallucination. "Glenn." Nothing else came out. Her senses and too many questions battled each other for first words. Any fool could see the man still looked swallow-your-tongue good. A little gray at the temples, a little more meat on his bones, but still tall, still fit, and still too handsome for his own good.

Glenn's attention shifted briefly from Eileen to Meg standing beside him, her brows arched in confusion, then back to Eileen. Letting his hands come to rest on the back of the chair, his eyes leveled with hers. "Mind if I join you?"

Her mouth still dry, Eileen gestured toward the chair he'd been leaning on.

Meg's eyes darted back and forth between the latest guest at her bed and breakfast and her husband's aunt. One smart cookie, Meg opted to have a seat, and rather than ask pointed questions, she continued to observe.

Settled into the ladder-back chair, Glenn leaned forward, talking over the music. "Would you ladies like another drink?"

Eileen shook her head and Meg mumbled, "No, thank you."

Turning in his seat, he waved down the waitress, ordered a dark beer, and spun around to face the two women.

Forcing a polite smile, Eileen gave words to the one question that had finally jockeyed into lead position, begging to be asked. "What are you doing here?"

The man she'd known so very well, so very long ago, leveled his gaze with hers. "I wrote you that I had business in Midland and was hoping to make time to stop by."

The letter still sitting in her dresser drawer.

"You didn't read the letter?" His pointed look told her that even after all these years, Glenn just might still be able to read her mind, or perhaps he'd simply become better at guessing.

"Why would I?" She lifted her chin and kept her gaze level with his. "I've gotten two letters from you in my lifetime. The first over twenty-five years ago didn't go over so well. I figured why play with fire."

Meg's eyes circled big and round and Eileen could almost see her efforts to connect the dots.

Despite the music playing behind them, Glenn lowered his voice. "I should have handled things better."

Of course he should have. After she'd postponed the wedding for the second time, he'd had the nerve to hang up on her. She'd been hurt and furious. What had he expected her to do? Her sister was gone and Eileen was the only mother her infant niece had come to know. Lord knows in those early days Sean had been so overwhelmed with grief he'd barely managed to put one foot in front of the other for the sake of the boys. The only one able to care for Grace the way Helen would have wanted had been her. And thank heaven for that. Grace had been Eileen's link to her sister, her salve for the heartbreaking grief. "I had my hands full."

"I hadn't understood." Glenn blew out a deep sigh. "At least, not then."

Meg waved the waitress over. "I've changed my mind. I think I may need another drink after all. Aunt Eileen?"

She shook her head.

"I have two daughters. Grown now." Glenn fingered the rim of his longneck. "As an infant, Charlotte had colic. I'd pace with her in the middle of the night, try and give Sally a break, but only her mother could ease her discomfort."

Eileen bit down hard. For Grace the hard time had been teething. Eileen paced alone many a night.

"Pacing, worrying, trying to make Charlotte feel better, well, sometimes I'd think of Grace. And how you must have felt." He paused, shifted in his seat and leveled his eyes with hers. "I'm sorry. I just didn't understand. Didn't know."

A plethora of comebacks danced on the tip of her tongue: too little too late, a day late and a dollar short, not worth a plug nickel. Swallowing the words, Eileen opted for the golden rule: if you can't say anything nice, don't say anything at all. "And how is Sally?"

His finger stilled. "We lost her almost three years ago."

"Oh, I'm sorry to hear that." She sank against the chair back. "Really sorry."

"I think," Meg's gaze followed the waitress juggling a tray of drinks two tables over, "I'll go get the drink from Jamie at the bar." Her questioning gaze bore into Eileen.

Of course she wouldn't leave without Eileen's assurance all would be fine. Forcing a brighter smile, she patted her niece's hand. "I've changed my mind as well. Ask Jamie to pick something for me."

"If you'll excuse me." Meg nodded and pushed away from the table.

The place was crowded. Not only were the locals standing elbow to elbow, there were plenty of new faces Eileen didn't recognize. Just like Jamie had predicted, a little reminiscent of the movie *Field of Dreams*, if he brought a taste of Ireland to Texas, folks scattered around the county would come. Who knew Glenn Baker would be one of them.

• • • •

Breathe, Glenn repeated to himself for the umpteenth time since deciding to step out of his room at the B&B in search of Eileen Callahan.

Stowed away in his room for the last few days, he'd thought he'd prepared himself for the reunion. Until he saw her sitting under the dimmed lights of the old pub. How, after all these years, could the sight of Eileen Callahan still strike him in the solar plexus like a pugilist's blow? She hadn't changed a bit. He also realized the reason she hadn't responded to him was plain and simple—she hadn't bothered to read the letter. And yet, despite the initially frosty reception, here she sat smiling at him.

Her gaze drifted to the band and then back to him.

"Do you miss it?" he asked.

"No." Then leaning back, she smiled. "Maybe sometimes. What about you? Are you still playing?"

He shook his head. "After our second daughter was born, I took a break from touring but we continued to do local gigs and studio sessions. With the girls only two years apart they didn't need a father on the road for weeks or months at a time. Then when Sally got sick, well, it was time to stop. She needed me more."

The light in Eileen's gaze dimmed and he knew exactly what she was thinking. That very concept was what she'd tried to explain to him when Grace was born. They needed her home, not on the road. He'd behaved like an ass and no amount of apologies would make up for that, but maybe fate had finally given him a chance to at least make it up to her a little.

"Here we go." The owner of the B&B reappeared, setting two glasses of wine on the table before retaking her seat.

Raising her glass to her niece, Eileen waited for him to do the same. "Sláinte."

The band chose that moment to shift from Irish to American tunes, starting with Neil Diamond's "Sweet Caroline." With the crowd chanting the chorus at the top of their lungs, conversation suddenly became near impossible without shouting. Call him fickle, but he didn't want the entire place to hear what he had to say. "Join me for coffee tomorrow?"

Leaning a fraction closer, she cupped her hand behind her ear. "Say that again?"

"Coffee," he said more strongly, "tomorrow. Join me?"

The way her eyes suddenly popped open he was pretty sure she'd heard him. Her gaze darted over to the bartender huddled with another guy staring at them, and back to him. He could see her chest rise with a deep intake of breath and fall again as she exhaled and nodded.

"Nine o'clock?"

"Make it ten. I've got morning chores and the ranch is nearly an hour away. Café is the only place in town at that hour."

Pushing to his feet, he couldn't help the grin that threatened to take over his face, before nodding and repeating, "Ten o'clock." Turning to Meg, he smiled at her too. "I'll see you in the morning."

"What about your dinner?" Meg asked.

Feeling ten feet tall and the weight of too many years easing from his shoulders, he wasn't the least bit in the mood to eat. "Guess I wasn't very hungry after all."

Another round of goodnights and he was out the door and making his way up the road to the B&B. So many possibilities had crossed his mind and done battle over what would happen when he came face to face with Eileen Callahan. The way she'd looked at him when he first sat down beside her, he'd expected to be wearing his drink before long. Bouncing up the porch steps Glenn had to admit one thing, tomorrow could prove to be one heck of a day for the record books.

● ● ● ●

Head in the fridge, Sean Farraday pulled out a stack of leftover storage tubs, slammed them on the counter and then one by one shoved them back into the refrigerator. Spinning on his boot heel he stomped to the extra fridge and in search of a beer, almost yanked the door off the hinges. Maybe bourbon was a better idea.

Storming back across the kitchen, he rounded the corner to the living room and almost crashed smack into his youngest son.

"Lose something?"

"No." He spun about. "Getting a late night snack."

"From the bar?" Always a man of few words, Finn crisscrossed the room. Gathering a pair of drinking glasses, a gallon of milk, a platter of his aunt's chocolate chip cookies and setting them on the table, he slid into a seat at the massive kitchen table.

Sean stood in the archway connecting the two rooms while Finn filled two glasses from the container. The kid had always been the voice of reason in the family regardless of any turmoil about. Sean didn't know if he'd been born that way or if it was something he'd had to learn in the midst of the chaos of losing his mother so young. Whatever the cause, right now the last thing Sean felt like doing was sitting down to milk and cookies. He wasn't six years old, and damn it if that wasn't part of his problem.

Shoving a full glass across the table, Finn dipped a cookie into his own glass. "You're making enough noise down here to wake the dead."

"I was hungry." He still wasn't used to having Finn and Joanna on the first floor. Only recently had they converted the guest rooms off the kitchen into a more private wing until they got around to building their own home on the property.

Finn nudged the glass of milk a few more inches in Sean's direction then took another bite of cookie.

"Damn infuriating." Without sitting down Sean took a long swig of the cool glass of milk. He'd rather have bourbon.

Swallowing the last bite of his cookie, Finn reached for another. "Want to tell me what has your chaps in a twist?"

"Told you. I'm hungry."

Finn nodded. "So this has nothing to do with the man at the pub tonight with Aunt Eileen?"

"He wasn't with her." At least not yet. The moment Meg told him the name of the man seated with Eileen, Sean saw red.

"Or is it that she mentioned meeting him again tomorrow that has you all bent out of shape?"

Whirling around, he waved a finger at his youngest son. "Do you have any idea at all who that man is?" Even to his own ears he could hear the gravely distress in his words.

"Can't say that I do."

"That man," Sean bit down on his back teeth, "is Glenn Baker."

Finn nodded. "That much we all heard. His name and that he's here for a short visit."

"Great," he muttered. "Just great."

"Sorry, Dad, you're losing me again. Want to start from the beginning?"

It wasn't his place to start from anywhere. Eileen was entitled to her privacy. He gulped down the last of the milk and slammed the glass down hard before remembering Joanna was probably trying to sleep. "No."

Forearms on the table, Finn leaned forward, shaking his head. "If this man is going to bring trouble to Aunt Eileen then you need to let us in. Farradays take care of Farradays."

Except Eileen wasn't a Farraday, she was a Callahan and if Helen hadn't died so young and he hadn't been so needy, Eileen would be a Baker now. No. Seething, he strode to the bar for the bourbon. That SOB should have waited for her. If Glenn had truly loved Eileen the way she deserved, he would have waited for her no matter how long it took. Showing up all these years later wasn't... fair. Not to anyone.

"Dad," Finn grabbed him by the arm, "you're scaring me. Who the hell is this guy?"

"He's the man who broke your aunt's heart."

CHAPTER TWO

Three in the morning was no time for Eileen to be dragging herself out of bed. Not even for a rancher, but there was no point in battling her pillow or counting a new herd of sheep. Last night had weighed on her mind and kept her tossing and turning. Not just the unexpected visit from the bloody Ghost of Christmas Past, but the prospect of seeing him again today and everything in between.

With the excitement over the success of the grand opening and Jamison's proposal to Abby, Glenn's name had barely been mentioned during the car ride home. That had suited her fine since she hadn't a clue what else to say anyhow.

Home, exhausted and a tad overwhelmed, she'd seen the questions in Sean's eyes and simply wasn't up to finding the answers. Instead she'd forgone her and Sean's nightly ritual of herbal tea before bed and gone straight to her room.

Later she'd heard him still rustling about in the kitchen and considered marching herself downstairs, but when Finn's voice carried to the upstairs hall, she'd closed her door and crawled back into bed. For all the good it had done her.

Showered and dressed in the near middle of the night, she'd packed a hearty lunch for her men, scrambled up some eggs and made breakfast burritos for later since she wouldn't be home when they got in from moving the cattle. Sitting in Sean's truck, she turned the key and the engine roared to life. The sound brought a smile to her face. Back in the day when she knew nothing at all about ranch life, the only thing she could think of to do for Sean was to warm his truck up from the bitter early morning air. The look of sheer appreciation and gratitude on his face had kept her turning it on through an awful lot of chilled mornings. Even though the night air had yet to reach below freezing, she'd come out here anyhow, and like it or not, it was time to go inside and face the music.

Back in the house, she filled the thermos with strong coffee and decided if ever there was a reason to call on the social club at this ungodly hour, Glenn was it.

"Morning." Sean came to a stop beside her and reached for the coffee pot.

Eileen pushed the empty mug closer to him. "Morning."

Keeping his gaze on his mug, he poured some cream. "Are we going to talk about him now?"

Almost relieved to have someone she trusted to bounce her thoughts and confusion off of, the words simply didn't come. She truly had no idea what to say to the man she'd helped to raise seven children. Discussing schoolyard spats, sibling rivalry, and higher education was a breeze. Telling him how her heart nearly stuttered to a stop as her past walked into her present—how could she? She'd barely shared two words about her and Glenn's relationship all those years ago, and now all she knew was that the man's daughter had colic as a baby and his wife had died. She didn't even know why Glenn had detoured to Tuckers Bluff. "I have things to do before meeting Glenn for coffee and I need to… to go now."

Lifting his cup, he turned to face her. His normally marble blue eyes had taken on the steely shade of a man with too much on his mind. His gaze shifted out the window into the darkness. No sign of dawn. The door to Finn and Joanna's rooms inched open and Sean poured another cup for his son, then turned to her. "Stay safe."

With a nod and deep breath, she grabbed her purse and keys, and clutching her phone, scurried out the door like a scared rabbit.

Despite the rancher's hour, her best friend picked up on the first ring and agreed to put on the coffee and call in the other ladies.

"All right. You got us here at the crack of dawn. Now spit it out." From her spot at the large table in Dorothy's kitchen, Sally Mae skewered Eileen with a piercing glare.

"Give the woman a chance to absorb some caffeine." Dorothy walked over with a fresh coffee pot in one hand.

Eileen held up an empty coffee cup and wondered what in the name of all that was holy had possessed her to call a meeting of the social club. Oh yeah, because her past had just risen from the dead and wanted to share a cup of coffee in—she looked at the clock on the wall—three hours.

Dorothy filled Eileen's cup and then moved to pour a mug for Sally Mae.

A car door slammed and a few seconds later Ruth Ann came huffing through the door and hurried into the kitchen. "I got here as fast as I could. Who's dying?"

"No one," three voices echoed.

Ruth Ann dumped her oversized purse in the nearest chair. Her mouth slightly agape, she looked from one friend to the other. "Well I know none of you are pregnant."

Any other time and Eileen would have laughed.

"Sit." Dorothy pointed to the chair in front of her with an empty coffee mug on the table and filled it, then filled her own and took a seat beside Eileen.

With three pairs of eyes on her, Eileen almost wished she'd just stayed in bed.

After a few long moments of silence Sally Mae put her cup on the table. "What'll it take for you to loosen your tongue and tell us what couldn't wait till the card game later today?"

"Where to start?" She wasn't really asking anyone else.

"Do you want us to start playing cards here or is this so bad we need to switch to the hard stuff?"

"This has something to do with the man staying at Meg's B&B, doesn't it?" Ruth Ann asked.

Eileen raised a brow. She shouldn't be surprised. Half the town saw her drinking with Meg and a stranger. Even though he'd left shortly after they'd agreed to meet this morning for coffee at the cafe—another stupid decision so that the whole town could watch them—all her nephews and a handful of friends had taken notice, though no one had had the nerve to come out and ask her about him.

Now that she was here at her dearest friend's house surrounded by the best friends a woman could ask for, she had no idea why she was behaving like a melodramatic teenager. So what if Glenn was here for a visit. Wanted to talk. Perhaps be friends again. Or maybe be more? *More.* That was what had her tossing and turning chasing sleep like the princess atop a mattress and one ridiculous pea.

"That does it." Sally Mae stood up. "Where are the cards? I'll deal."

Maybe the woman was right. Having something to do with her hands would make this easier. Put things into perspective.

Five minutes later three of them sat around a table, playing cards in hand. Dorothy stood holding out a bottle of Baileys. "A little Irish in anyone's coffee?"

All three held up their cups.

Dorothy smiled. "Thought so."

Seated and rearranging her cards, Dorothy was the first to speak. "I'm in. I'll take two and who is he?"

"I'll take one." Ruth Ann tossed in a chip. "A guest at Meg's B&B."

Sally Mae dealt Dorothy's and Ruth Ann's cards. "He's more than that. I saw the look in his eyes when the lights came on after the music was done, but Roy shuffled me out of there before I could find out."

"You saw him?" Ruth Ann asked. "How did I miss it?"

Dorothy shuffled her cards around in her hand. "Because you and Ralph never got off the dance floor long enough to notice anything."

"How would you know?" Sally Mae narrowed her eyes at her longtime friend. "You weren't even there."

"I know. I hated to miss it, but when the Bradys asked me to babysit so they could go, well, I figured it was more for the young. They may have mentioned all the canoodling." Dorothy laid her cards face down on the table. "So, I repeat, who is he?"

"Glenn Baker." Staring at her hand, Eileen tossed a chip in the pot. "I'll have three cards and there was no canoodling."

Nothing happened. No cards were dealt. No chips hit the pot. No sounds.

Eileen looked up from her cards. All three women stared at her, mouths hanging open.

Snapping her mouth shut, Dorothy poured more Baileys into her coffee. "I might need something stronger."

"What's *he* doing here?" Sally Mae asked. "I mean now. After all these years."

"Yeah." Ruth Ann put her cards down. "Why now?"

All the same questions that had crossed her mind. "Sally, his wife, died."

"So he comes running to you?" Dorothy picked her cards back up then slammed them down again. "Talk about too little too late."

"The gall." Ruth Ann fanned her cards again. "Who does he think you are?"

Her mouth pursed like she'd sucked on a lemon, Sally Mae shook her head, dealt herself a card, and mumbled, "Should be run out of town on a rail."

"Works for me," Dorothy agreed and tossed a chip into the pot. "I'm in for five."

Ruth Ann tossed a chip in the pot with a little more force than was needed, setting the makeshift pot to teetering. "I'm in and willing to donate feathers."

"Ladies," Eileen tossed in a chip, "don't you think you're getting a little carried away? It's not like he compromised my virtue at the turn of the last century or shot my lover in cold blood."

"Might as well have," Ruth Ann muttered.

"He should have understood you were needed here. Been willing to give you time. At least talked it out. Something."

"That's right," Dorothy added. "It's not like just anyone could step into a household of seven children and a grieving father and make it all better in a few weeks."

"It was months," Eileen said softly.

"So?" Sally Mae said.

"Maybe," Eileen put her cards down, "if I'd let him come." When Helen had gotten so sick from the infection Eileen hadn't been worried. Doctors and medicine cured infections all the time. Eileen hadn't realized how many women still died in childbirth, even in this day and age. The shock and pain had been nearly unbearable, and yet, when Glenn had said he'd catch the next flight. Come. Be with her. Help. She'd said no. She'd reminded him that the band was just getting a name for themselves. People were starting to recognize them—him. The upcoming gigs were important. He had to do them. Couldn't step away.

"We went over this twenty something years ago," Dorothy said. "It wasn't your fault. Even if he didn't come, he didn't have to marry the other singer."

"No." She picked up her cards. "He wanted to bring Gloria up to sing for me. Did I mention that?"

"Probably," Ruth Ann said.

Eileen nodded. "He did. I told him Sally had the stronger voice. She was the better replacement for me."

"On stage, honey." Sally Mae slammed the cards again. "Not in life."

"He apologized."

All eyes shifted toward her. Sally Mae was the one to fold her cards and face Eileen down. "Saying you're sorry you left the barn door open isn't going to get the horses back."

"What do barns and horses have to do with his walking out on her?" Ruth Ann asked.

Sally Mae rolled her eyes. "It's a metaphor. The horses or the barn aren't important. The point is the apology is too late."

"I don't know." Eileen laid her cards face up on the table. "Two pair."

"It's my turn to go first." Dorothy laid her cards down. "Three of a kind and what do you mean you don't know?"

What did she mean? The words, even all these years later, had been good to hear. Had made her feel…not vindicated…not exactly better, after all it had been over twenty-five years since they'd broken up, but somehow she felt…lighter.

"I don't like that look." Sally Mae laid her cards down, face up. "Full house."

"It's my turn," Ruth Ann grumbled. "Not that it matters, your full house beats my two pair aces high." Her hands stilled and she turned to face Eileen. "Wait. What look?"

Dorothy sighed. "The one that says she's forgiven him."

"She has?" Ruth Ann asked. "Why?"

"Forgive, shmorgive." Sally Mae gathered the cards on the table into a pile. "He could have apologized over the phone. Like twenty years ago."

"I'll give him this much," Dorothy helped collect the cards, "it says something for him that he came in person, but I don't know that I like that look in your eyes either."

"I don't have a look. And now that we've talked it out, I don't know why I'm making such a big deal of having a cup of coffee with him."

"You're having coffee?" Ruth Ann asked.

Eileen nodded. "Today at ten at the cafe. He wants to talk to me about something."

"He'd better not think you've just been sitting around waiting for him to waltz back into your life and sweep you off your feet." Sally Mae passed the deck to Dorothy to shuffle. "Your life is here. With your friends and your family."

Her life. Once upon a time, her life had been on a stage with the talented man of her dreams. Once upon a time.

● ● ● ●

"Testing. One, two, three. Oh say can you see…" Fancy's soft voice came through the speakers loud and clear. This would be Tow the Line's first gig in the new country music hall and she was more than a little nervous.

"Sounds good." Their soundman removed the headsets and set them down. "Fans are going to love this place."

"Yes." She couldn't agree more. The last year had been a whirlwind of mind boggling success. Two years ago, if anyone had asked her where she saw herself in the future, lead female singer for a chart-topping country music band would not have been her answer.

"You okay?" Garrett, an original member of Tow the Line, asked.

"Me? Sure."

"Don't tell me you're nervous about tonight? They're going to love the new songs."

"I know that. No one writes songs like Gil. The man is a musical genius."

"Agreed. They'll love his songs and they'll love you."

Would they? Sometimes she felt like such an imposter. "Maybe."

"Hey," that low dreamy voice that had wooed fans for years spoke softly, soothing her uneasy nerves. She would never have made it this far without his friendship. "Have you changed your mind?"

"How do you do that? Sometimes I feel like you're inside my brain." Shaking her head, she flashed him her best effort at a smile. "It's just... We're getting closer."

"We are. Have you told your sister you're coming yet?"

"Not exactly."

Garrett's brows lifted, making his already big blue eyes seem enormous. "Exactly what have you told her?"

"I sent a birthday card to Brittany and mentioned I'd hoped to see her soon."

Those two brows inched slightly higher. "So your sister has no idea you're on your way or what you want?"

She shook her head. Some habits die hard. Talking to her sister hadn't come easily since she was twelve, before her mother died.

"Fancy," he shifted around to face her, "you have been sending postcards for months but haven't spoken to Allison once. Don't you think she deserves to know what's going on in that pretty little head of yours?"

This time hers were the brows to shoot up high. "This is all so...hard..." Her voice trailed off and crossing her arms, she roughly brushed away a nonexistent chill. Would she ever get things right from the start? Outside of singing, she didn't seem to be able to do anything right. Well, maybe one thing. Brittany Farraday.

CHAPTER THREE

"Now remember," Dorothy rested her hand on Eileen's arm, "if you need anything, if you don't like where the conversation is going, you tug on your ear and we'll come running."

"That's right," Sally Mae agreed.

The Tuckers Bluff Afternoon Ladies Social Club gathered at their usual table in the Silver Spurs Café. Leaving Eileen out of this hand, the women played poker the same way they had week in and week out since before Eileen had come to live in Tuckers Bluff. Except now each of them kept one eye on the door and the other on the clock, waiting for Eileen's ten o'clock coffee date to appear.

Every time the old-fashioned over-the-door bell rang, the players would nonchalantly glance up. So far Ned the mechanic—who was older than dirt—had sauntered in and taken up his usual spot at the counter for his mid-morning libation. Polly from the Cut N Curl had run in as though her tail were on fire and picked up four cups of coffee to go. "You're a life saver. I suppose every coffee pot has a life span but I wish ours hadn't picked the busiest morning of the week to sputter and die."

"Next time just call and I can get someone to run it over," Abbie called to the woman's back as she practically sprinted out the door. But still no sign of Glenn.

Eileen glanced at the clock. Still five minutes to go. Maybe she should have played this round. Give her something to do besides kibitz and wait.

The bell sounded again and not until Dorothy muttered, "Oh my," did Eileen turn around. "If you don't want him, let me know. I'll take him."

"Dorothy!" Ruth Ann spat out.

"Hey, don't Dorothy me. You and Sally Mae have someone to keep you warm at night."

"Really," Sally Mae mumbled, shaking her head.

Eileen didn't say a word. She stood and sucking in a deep breath, propelled herself forward. She wasn't walking the plank. This was a simple catch up conversation with an old friend. Nothing more.

At first Glenn looked around, his stance stiff, his gaze searching. As soon as he spotted Eileen walking toward him, his shoulders eased and a lazy smile she still remembered spread from cheek to cheek.

Abbie came rushing over to the new customer, a menu in hand, and nearly tipped forward screeching to a halt when Eileen stepped up beside him.

"Morning," Eileen said softly.

"Morning, Leeni." Glenn met Abbie's confused gaze. "Table for two, please."

"Someplace quiet. Maybe a booth," Eileen added.

Abbie's gaze bounced from Glenn to Eileen to the row of empty booths and seemed to work extra hard to make her mouth move. "Follow me."

Eileen did her best to pretend every eye in the place wasn't watching her.

"Frank's lunch special is ready early today. Chicken Cacciatore and the pie is Boston Cream." Her gaze darting over to Eileen and back, Abbie handed a menu to Glenn. She took his drink order and snuck a sideways glance at Eileen. Pulling a couple of napkins from her apron, setting them on the table and casting one more inquisitive look in Eileen's direction, she announced, "I'll be back in a jiff with your drinks and to take your orders."

"Thank you, Abbie." Eileen did her best to offer Jamison's—as of last night—fiancée a casual, all-is-well-with-the-world smile and prayed it didn't look like she was about to heave her breakfast.

"Meg's been telling me all about the Farradays," Glenn started.

"She has?"

"I've been in town for a couple of days." A hint of pink tinged his cheeks. "I was working up my nerve. Anyhow, at breakfast at least one of your nephews, or their wives, came up in conversation. By last night I pretty much realized what all the boys and Grace have grown up to be and I discovered there are three more cousins."

"Actually there are another six, but we don't get to see them very often. Hannah, Ian and Jamison are Sean's cousin Brian's brood. They were raised here in Texas. Not far from Austin. Brian's brother Patrick did a bit of wandering before he finally settled down in Wyoming."

"And you're Aunt Eileen to all of them?"

She nodded. Even though Brian and Patrick's clans had no true relation to Eileen, she'd been their aunt as much as she'd been one to her sister's children.

"Hey." Jamison, Brian's eldest son, strolled up to the table and leaned over to give his aunt a kiss on the cheek. "How's it going?"

"Fine." Eileen smiled, she knew what her nephew was up to. No doubt Abbie had texted him about Eileen's coffee companion the second Abbie had crossed through the kitchen double doors. "What brings you about at this hour?"

"Oh." Jamie's gaze lifted to the view of his cousin's clinic across the street, clearly surprised at his aunt's intentional failure to introduce him. "Heard Boston Cream was on the menu today. Thought I'd come get me a mid-morning pick me up."

"Uh, huh." Eileen nodded.

"Anyway," Jamie's gaze danced from his aunt to her companion and back, "I'd better get going before the pie's all gone."

"You do that." Eileen smiled, watching her nephew walk backwards a few steps before turning around and greeting his fiancée at the counter with a big fat kiss. Not a surprise considering young love and all.

"He was working the bar last night, right?"

"Yes, O'Fearadaigh's was Jamie's brain child." Shaking off her thoughts of Jamie and Abbie, and his sudden appearance this morning, Eileen smiled at Glenn. "Tell me about your girls. Two, you said?"

"That's right. They're the reason I began looking up old friends. They insisted—"

"Hello." Declan came to a halt in full uniform at his aunt's side. "Thought you'd be playing cards this morning."

Eileen glanced around her police chief nephew to look for a guilty expression on Abbie's face. Was the woman planning on alerting every one of the nephews about her companion this morning?

"I was taking a coffee break."

"I see." DJ turned to face the man sitting across from her.

"I'm Glenn Baker." His hand shot out. "Nice to meet you."

DJ nodded. "Chief Farraday."

Oh, the communications this morning from Abbie must have been a doozie for DJ to introduce himself with his official moniker. What did he think, that Glenn was here to shanghai her into a sex slave ring?

"I hear the Boston Cream is pretty good. Why don't you get a slice to take back to Esther? That woman works too hard." The suggestion was about as subtle as Eileen could manage at this point.

DJ's one brow lifted higher than the other.

"As a matter of fact," Eileen waved a finger in Abbie's direction, "you should take a piece to Reed at the station. Isn't he on duty this morning?" Of course Eileen already knew that because not an hour ago the other officer had come in for a cup of coffee before heading out to patrol the outskirts of the town. Since her nephew didn't seem to be in any hurry to move, she smiled up at him. "Thanks for stopping by."

"Yes. Guess I'll get some of that pie you suggested."

Waiting a few beats, she kept an eye on DJ until he was at least out of earshot. If the man moved any slower he wouldn't make it back to the police station before next spring. Facing Glenn again, she blew out a breath. "You were saying?"

He glanced over her shoulder, either considering what to say next or perhaps searching for where the conversation had left off. "Where were we?"

"Your daughters are the reason…"

"Yes." He nodded and paused as Abbie set a cup of coffee in front of each of them.

"Would you two be wanting to eat something?"

"Actually," Glenn flashed the charming smile he'd used often to get his way, "a piece of that Boston Cream pie everyone's talking about sounds pretty good."

Abbie nodded and turned to Eileen. "And you, Aunt Eileen?"

"Make that two with a dollop of whipped cream on mine."

"Got it. Two pies coming up."

Glenn leaned forward, elbows on the table. "As I said, Sally passed three years ago and I'll be honest, that first year I was in a haze."

Eileen nodded. She knew exactly what he meant. Even though she'd been kept on her toes with a new baby and an energetic crew of six boys, there had been a thin layer of fog filling her brain for a long time after she lost her sister.

He continued, "Earlier this year, they sat me down and said I needed to get out of my rut. I hadn't considered my life a rut, but two years had passed and my girls' persistent nagging to rejoin the living got me to realize how lost I'd been. It hadn't taken much more persuasion on their part to convince me reaching out to old friends would be a good thing."

"And that's why you're here?" Heaven knew she'd lost enough sleep last night wondering why now.

"Part of it. You see, I've also been looking up—"

"Morning." Finn took off his hat, smacked it on his side, and grinned at his aunt.

There was way too much smiling and grinning going on, and absolutely no reason for Finn to be in town today. All she'd told her brother-in-law and nephew on the ride home last night was that she'd be meeting Glenn for coffee today. She didn't mention what time or if they'd be staying in town or driving to Butler Springs. Unless—her gaze darted to Abbie across the cafe and she practically groaned, slapping her hands flat on the table. "That's enough."

"Finnegan Farraday." Finn extended his hand to Glenn, ignoring his aunt's little outburst. "Folks call me Finn."

Eileen shook a finger at Finn and the others. "We're not going to do this with every member of the family. Finn, this is Glenn, an old friend who is passing through town," she paused to look at Glenn, who nodded, "and we're just catching up a bit over coffee and pie. That's it. Nothing else. I'm not at risk to be Shanghaied."

"What?" Glenn looked up.

Eileen shook her head and waved off the comment. "Never mind, I just want you to spread the—"

"Morning." Sean Farraday maneuvered around his youngest son, but unlike the others who stood awkwardly at the table, he slid into the booth beside her, folding his hands on the table at the same moment Abbie walked up with two slices of pie. "Oh, that looks good. I'll have the same."

For the first time since Glenn had come through the door, Abbie smiled brightly. "Another piece of pie coming right up."

The bell over the door sounded and Eileen didn't dare look up, but like passing a train wreck near the highway, she simply couldn't resist. Sauntering in their direction, Brooks came her way. Stopping to slap his brother DJ on the back before the two of them, accompanied by Jamie, came her way. Again.

"Morning." Brooks flashed a smile at his aunt and slapped his brother Finn the same way he had DJ.

Eileen scanned the men in front of her from left to right. "Doesn't anyone work for a living anymore?"

"Man's gotta eat." Brooks shrugged one shoulder. "Actually, just came from making rounds at the hospital. I was meeting my wife for a late breakfast when I spotted you."

Sure, she believed that one. He probably wanted to sell her a waterfront property in the desert. Not that she didn't expect his wife to come by any minute as explained, but they no more met for breakfast on a Friday morning than she had tea with the Queen. "You'll have to get your own booth. This one's full."

"Are you expecting someone else?" Finn pointed to the empty spot beside Glenn.

"No," Glenn's response tumbled over Eileen's, "Yes."

Finn looked from one person at the table to the other and hesitated.

"Here you go." Abbie shouldered past the Farraday men hovering around the booth and set a plate of Boston Cream pie in front of Sean and facing Finn, set a blueberry slice in front of the empty spot beside Glenn. "I know you like blueberry better so I brought you that instead." Still smiling, she turned back to the others. "More coffee coming right up."

With her brother-in-law installed at her side and her nephew now shrugging into the seat across the table, Eileen didn't see any way out of this without making a scene. She should have suggested having coffee in Butler Springs. Except for one little tiny thing—she wasn't sure she was ready to spend a few hours confined in a car with the man she'd once thought she would marry. Until she'd opened that letter and learned he'd married someone else.

• • • •

For a few minutes Sean was sure Eileen was going to kick him out of the booth. Or maybe clear out of the state of Texas. Not that she didn't have good reason to. He had no business barging in on her reunion. After all, who she spent her time with was her own business. In all these years he'd never overstepped his bounds and now was no time to start. And yet, something deep inside wouldn't let him get up and leave.

Most likely that something was the way this man across the table smiled at her as if she were a prize rodeo buckle. Or maybe it was the memory of those first nights after this same man had called off the wedding with a single slamming down of the phone. More than once he had passed by Eileen's room on the way to his own and could hear her quiet sobs. He hadn't known what to do or say. How to make it better. Even though he hadn't a clue how he'd get along without her help, he'd encouraged her to go back to her own dreams.

When she made it clear that Grace and the boys came first no matter the cost, he'd wanted to throttle the man with his bare hands for being unwilling to wait. How could he not have given her the time they all needed? How much could this musician have loved her not to wait a little longer? And then the ultimate betrayal only a few months later. There would be no forgetting her valiant efforts to bat back tears as she scanned the contents of that blasted letter. Someone else was singing her songs, married to her love, living her dream. She deserved more than this man years ago, and she certainly deserved more than him now.

• • • •

Except for Finn who had eased his way into the booth with his father, once Eileen read the riot act, any and all relatives were immediately dispatched across the café. Despite the distance, Glenn could feel each pair of eyes boring into the back of his head. The Farraday clan were as close to them now as if Eileen had invited them to pull up a chair and join the table.

Which brought him back to the man seated in front of him. Last night Glenn had been prepared for the possibility that Eileen would throw him and his apology into a pit of slithering rattlers. He had not expected the piercing glare throwing daggers his way from Sean Farraday. Now, more than two decades after the implosion of his and Eileen's engagement, Glenn more than understood he could have handled things differently. All right, better. His first mistake had probably been not coming for the funeral despite Eileen's objections. Maybe then if he'd seen for himself he would have understood. Been more patient. *Or not.* In the end he'd come to believe he could not compete with her sister's children. Or maybe he'd simply been afraid to really try. None of which mattered any more. What he needed now was a few minutes alone with Eileen. He hadn't been this excited about anything in years and not until last night did he realize just how much Eileen still mattered. He very much wanted her to be excited too.

CHAPTER FOUR

L istening to Finn pepper Glenn with questions under the guise of conversation, Eileen wondered first: when did her quiet, pensive nephew become so talkative, and second: what would happen if she stabbed someone with a fork? Any more politely stiff conversation and she might just stab *herself* with a fork to get the day over with.

"So, this is your first time in Texas?" Finn asked.

"No." Glenn fiddled with the last bite of pie on his plate. "But it's been many years since we played in Texas."

"Played?" Finn's brows crinkled. "You're an athlete?"

Glenn tipped his head back with laughter. "Hardly. I'm a jazz pianist."

"And a dang good one." A familiar sense of pride bubbled inside her. "At least, you used to be."

"Still am, thank you. Even if I haven't played for an audience since…" His words trailed off and his hands stilled momentarily before he stabbed at the last piece and forced a smile in Eileen's direction. "Do you remember the Blue Tortoise?"

The name seemed vaguely familiar. It had been so many years since they'd performed together. Always on the road, from town to town, night after… "Wait. Wasn't that in Austin? The club with the huge stuffed turtle—right?"

"Tortoise. Yes. And between sets the waitresses would get up on the bars and do those hand jive moves."

"That's right. I remember. They booked us a couple of times." Content in the memory, Eileen leaned back, her arm barely brushing against Sean's as she relaxed a bit for the first time since the Farraday clan arrived. "The owner's favorite song was—"

"Miss Otis Regrets." Glenn eased his head from side to side grinning. "Some nights I'd lose track of how many times he'd have you sing that song."

"Some nights I wondered if he'd let us get in a whole set without it. Though I did often wonder why he seemed so fond of the woman who strayed on lovers' lane and pulled a gun from under her velvet gown."

"One of Cole Porter's more entertaining tunes." Glenn chuckled.

Finn opened and closed his mouth a few times before finally spitting out, "You sang? I mean, professionally?"

"Don't look so horrified." Eileen felt indignation inch up her spine.

"Your voice was—is—golden." For the first time since Finn began his ill-disguised attempt at casual questions, Sean entered the conversation, sharing that barely there lift to one side of his mouth that almost all his sons had inherited. "You just don't sing much any more."

She shook her head. Give her a few glasses of wine and a really big party and she couldn't resist. At just about every Farraday wedding over the last year or so, at some point she'd picked up a mic and sung to her hearts content.

"How did I not know this?" Finn leaned forward, resting his arms on the table. "I mean, I know you and Aunt Anne can sing all night but... wait. Did Aunt Anne used to sing professionally too? Were y'all some sort of girls' singing group?"

Eileen swallowed a laugh. "Don't know many jazz girls' singing groups. And no, your aunt has a fabulous voice, but except for a wedding or two, she's never set foot on a stage."

"Did you know?" Fin looked to his dad.

"How could I not know?" Finn's father bobbed his head. "Your mother was so very proud that she would play their album over and over and over. I'm surprised she didn't wear it out."

Eileen turned her head sideways staring at her brother-in-law "I didn't know that. I didn't even know she had a copy."

"Yep," Sean set his fork down on the cleaned pie plate. "We probably still have it."

As much as Eileen loved singing and music, once she took over raising Grace and the boys there was no time for playing with the stereo. Honestly, she had no idea what record albums Helen and Sean might have had. It had probably just been easier for her that way.

Once again Finn's jaw fell slightly open before he snapped it shut to speak. "You made an album?"

"Just one," she said.

Glenn raised a finger. "Actually, almost two."

"What do you mean almost two?"

"You know how difficult Slim was on that first production—"

Eileen nodded. "For all I knew all producers were like that."

"Not really, but we didn't know any better. Anyhow, two of the recordings didn't make it on that first album. Our new producer thought they were phenomenal and added them to the second album." Glenn leaned back in the booth. "There were releases that had to be signed. You must have seen them and signed them and sent them back, or the songs wouldn't have been on the album."

Somewhere in the recesses of her mind, Eileen had a vague recollection of receiving a stack of paperwork from the record company's attorney. At that point in her life she'd signed anything that hinted at receiving royalties.

"So let me see if I understand this," Finn waved a hand from his aunt to the man beside him, "you guys were famous enough to record multiple albums?"

Eileen pointed at Glenn. "Not while I was with the band. We were just starting out. Mostly on a wing and a prayer. Besides, Glenn had the magic fingers that could make any keyboard sound like music from heaven. I always knew the unconventional way he used meters would get the band noticed."

"Wow." Finn leaned back. "Just wow."

Abbie appeared, a pot of coffee in her hand. "Anybody for another cup?"

"I need to pick up an order at the feed store and get back to the ranch." Finn shook his head and placing his hands flat on the table, pushed to his feet then swung his gaze to his father. "You want me to pick you up on my way back to the ranch?"

Sean looked at his son then shifted his attention to Glenn and back to Eileen. She'd been reading this man for over twenty years, knew what he was thinking as clearly as her own thoughts, and yet, at this moment she didn't have a clue what all the emotions lingering behind those steel blue eyes were all about.

"We've got a ranch to run, we had better get going. This is on me." With little more than a nod to Eileen and a wave to Abbie, Sean followed his son to the register.

Eileen glanced across the way to see that the table of relatives had cleared. Lost in conversation and the past, she hadn't even noticed when they'd gotten up. On the other hand, the social club was still playing cards. To anyone else in the place the ladies looked to be intent in their poker hands, but Eileen could see the furtive glances cast sporadically in her direction.

"The family is quite close, I see."

For a fraction of a moment, she'd almost forgotten Glenn was sitting across from her. "Yes," she nodded, "yes, they are." Visions of all the Farraday's, their other halves, and still another generation working in the kitchen, filling the enormous dining room table, and even now showing up uninvited, the togetherness made her smile. She'd done good. Well, she and Sean had.

● ● ● ●

All it had taken was one text from Finn to have almost every Farraday in Tuckers Bluff gathered around the kitchen at Meg's or on their way.

"All right." Meg was the first to speak up. "I'll admit I'm extremely curious to know what's going on. This is seriously out of the norm for your aunt."

Adam stood behind his wife, looping his arms around her waist. "All any of the patients at the vet clinic this morning could talk about was Aunt Eileen and the new stranger, who apparently isn't much of a stranger."

"I'm as curious as the next guy, but if we're going to talk about Aunt Eileen, shouldn't she be here? Or at least Dad?" Becky leaned against DJ.

Brooks looked to Finn. "Where is Dad?"

"While we were at the feed store, Ken Brady came in to pick up some parts for his skid steer that jammed up again. Since Dad can work those contraptions in his sleep, he offered to go help. It's only a two man job so I told him I'd pick him up on my way home."

Meg sat on a nearby stool. "Does he know we're all meeting here?"

"No," Finn said. "I just thought this would be a good time to get most of us in the same place without Dad and Aunt Eileen."

"Why?" Brooks asked.

"I'm sure Aunt Eileen is going to get around to telling all of us herself, maybe, but in the meantime I figured it's best to get everyone up to speed. Starting with how I found Dad really ticked off last night, slamming things around in the kitchen and then this morning Aunt Eileen must have said something to him because he suggested we take the morning to come pick up our feed order instead of waiting for Chase to bring it tomorrow. And as most of you know, we wound up at the café. Let's wait for Ethan and Allison and—"

"Okay," Grace blew in the front door, with her husband Chase on her heels, "what is going on that can't wait until Sunday supper tomorrow?"

"Still waiting on Ethan," Finn said. "Don't want to say things twice."

"What about Connor?" Adam asked.

Finn shrugged. "I'll have to fill him in later."

The front door squeaked open and shut, bringing Ethan and his wife into the room. "We're here."

"Me, too." Toni waved at everyone and spotting Brooks, sidled up next to her husband.

"I wish I'd known we were going to have such a crowd." Meg pushed to stand and made her way to the fridge, pulling out cold cuts, cheeses and condiments. "Do-it-yourself sandwiches are now on the lunch menu."

Looping his arm around Toni's waist, Brooks gave his wife a quick peck on the lips. "Don't worry, we all ate something at the café."

"Oh, yeah," Meg muttered, then frowned at her two sisters-in-law. "Who's with Brittany and baby Helen?"

"Aunt Eileen," Toni answered.

"Aunt Eileen?" Several voices echoed so loudly Toni actually took a step back.

Toni glanced up at Brooks and back. "I told her that I was

invited to a last minute gathering and could she please cover for me with the kids. And," she looked to Finn, "I don't suppose this meeting has something to do with the man who is now helping our aunt babysit?"

Finn blew out a sigh. "Unless she's hiding another man in the closet, yes."

"So not surprised." Toni eased onto a stool near the island.

Not having made it to the café this morning, Adam reached for a loaf of bread. "You have the floor, little brother."

"As I was saying," Finn started, "Dad was really sore last night after this guy showed up at the pub and sat down with Aunt Eileen."

"It was a little weird." Meg slathered mustard on her bread. "One minute my guest was popping in for a bite to eat and the next minute he was calling Aunt Eileen Leeni and asking how she was doing."

"Leeni?" several voices echoed.

"That's what I'm talking about." Finn waved away Becky's attempt to hand him a sandwich. "Last night Dad was fuming because of who this guy is."

"And who is he?" Meg looked up from slicing a tomato.

"Aunt Eileen's ex fiancé."

If Finn weren't so concerned about this turn of events, he would have laughed at the number of jaws hanging open.

"Apparently," Finn continued, "they broke things off when she chose to stay at the ranch after Mom died."

Eyes popping open wide, most of Finn's siblings looked like a flock of spooked owls.

"Yeah." Finn ran his hand across the back of his neck. "I had no idea either. And here's another tidbit of news. Glenn is a jazz pianist and Aunt Eileen was his band's singer."

Mouths that had snapped shut fell open again. Meg spun away from the island and crossed the kitchen to open her laptop. Keyboard clacking, all eyes were on her. Nobody seemed to be able to find anything to say.

"Holy…" She whirled around. "This guy is actually a renowned jazz pianist known for his unusual use of meters—"

"Aunt Eileen said something about that at the café."

"He's played with Ella Fitzgerald—"

A few of his siblings whistled.

"Diana Krahl…" Meg continued to read off a list of who's who in the jazz world as scattered, *wow, you're kidding*, and more whistles were tossed around.

Ethan scrubbed his face. "This is surreal. You're telling me Aunt Eileen gave up the man she was going to marry for us?"

"Looks like it." Finn hefted one shoulder in a half-hearted shrug.

"And now he's back?" Brooks added.

DJ stood in the corner, arms and ankles crossed. "You think he's come back for her after all these years to what, steal her away?"

"Listen to this," Meg interrupted. "He had a wife who passed away three years ago from ALS. She was diagnosed eleven years ago. Right around the time Glenn disappeared from the music scene."

"So he stopped playing music to care for his wife." Ethan leaned back against the counter. "Sounds like a nice enough guy. Not someone we'd need to worry about with our aunt."

"Wait." Meg waved at Ethan. "The plot thickens. Glenn Baker and his lead singer Sally Marshall were married exactly eleven months after Grace was born."

"Didn't waste any time, did he?" Brooks scoffed.

DJ pushed away from the counter he'd been leaning against. "Doesn't look like it."

"Okay." Ethan tensed. "Maybe not that nice."

"Something doesn't smell right." Brooks shook his head. "Let's say Aunt Eileen broke up with him—"

"Dad said he broke her heart so I don't think that's what happened," Finn explained.

Brooks leaned forward on the island. "Now it down right stinks. He breaks the engagement with Aunt Eileen and then winds up marrying someone else pretty quickly. Awfully convenient if you ask me."

"That's my thought. If he couldn't be trusted back then, why should we trust him now?" Finn looked to his brother. "On the other hand, all I want is for Aunt Eileen to be happy, and believe it or not, by the time Dad and I left the café earlier, she looked happier than I remember seeing her in years."

"Of course she was." Adam chuckled. "She lives to boss us

around."

"True," Finn smiled, "but I think there's more to it."

"If this guy has come back for Aunt Eileen and he makes her happy, then I'm all for it." Adam leaned back against the counter and crossed his arms.

Meg held her hand up. "I love you, honey, but let's not go jumping to conclusions. There could be any number of reasons Glenn is here, and we have no way of knowing if he's here for her, or some other reason, or if having him in her life again is something she even wants."

Silence hung for a few moments as Meg's words sank in. As far as Finn was concerned, he wanted his aunt happy, but he'd rather have her happy in Tuckers Bluff.

"I'm not convinced it's any of our business." Toni stole a slice of baked ham from the countertop. "She is a grown woman, after all. She has a right to do whatever she wants with whomever she wants."

A few of the brothers squeezed their eyes shut, one of them mumbled, "TMI."

"Let's not get carried away here." Finn raised his hand. "It's not like we're going to lock her up in a chastity belt—"

Adam groaned. "I seriously don't need these images in my head."

"You're a vet," Finn shot back. "You deal with animal husbandry all day long."

"Yes, but none of those animals is like a mother to me, thank you very much."

Meg giggled and wrapped an arm around her husband's waist. "That's all right, sweetie. We'll just have to get your mind on something else."

Adam's nostrils flared and not a soul in the room doubted where his mind had just gone.

"Maybe I should dig a little deeper," DJ suggested.

The brothers looked from one to another. Pushing away from the counter behind him, Finn nodded. "Whatever you do, don't let Aunt Eileen find out, or no matter how old we are, none of us will be able to sit for a week." That made a few of his brothers laugh under their breaths.

"So now what?" Adam asked. "We just hang around and wait?"

Finn nodded. "And in the meantime, keep an eye on the man."

Brooks sighed. "So, we're laying odds that after all these years, he's come back for the one that got away?"

"That's my best bet." Finn had kicked this around since his Dad's tirade last night, again this morning at home, and later at the café. Nothing else made sense. If all he'd wanted was to catch up, that's what the internet or phone was for. A face to face meeting? Halfway across the country? "I mean, what else could make the man travel all the way to the middle of West Texas?"

CHAPTER FIVE

"**S**he seems quite taken with you." Holding Brittany on her hip, Eileen kept an eye on Glenn making funny faces at little Helen, who kept a firm grip on his nose.

"Remind me again. This is...?" He squinted his eyes in concentration.

Eileen smothered a soft laugh. "That's Brooks' and Toni's little girl. Brittany here belongs to Ethan and Allison."

"That's right. They're both so easy going. And this one... I don't remember either of my girls being this fascinated with my nose."

For a few seconds Eileen allowed a pang of regret to steal her breath. Had things worked out differently, would she and Glenn have had daughters? Sons? Would they have been as fascinated as her sister's namesake was at this very moment? "It's very nice of you to tag along. I'm sure you didn't come to West Texas to babysit."

Glenn chuckled and Helen let go of his nose, now drawn to the embroidery on his pocket. "I have to admit, this wasn't what I expected, but I'm glad to meet more of your family."

Ignoring another pang of regret, she shoved aside the memories of all the times he'd not wanted to meet her family and did her best to keep the mood light. "What, wasn't half the Farraday brood enough for you this morning?"

"Well," he cleared his throat, "I'll admit it was occasionally a bit intimidating. Sean didn't say much, but I was not sensing a lot of warm and fuzzy feelings from him."

"No." Eileen set Brittany down in the corral and handed her a graham cracker to gnaw on. Sean Farraday was a kind, considerate, thoughtful man with a devotion to friends and family worth its weight in gold. If a person needed boosting, the man always had a kind word or gracious smile or helping hand at the ready. There wasn't a soul in the county who didn't know they could count on Sean Farraday and his sons when needed. None of that was obvious from the man almost brooding beside her earlier today. Not since after his wife died had she seen so much darkness in his eyes.

"You okay?" Glenn placed Helen on the floor beside her cousin.

"Sorry, my mind wanders from time to time." Eileen took a seat on the sofa, one eye on the girls, one eye on Glenn. So much in this man had changed and yet remained the same. That impish smile still tugged at her heart strings, yet there was something calmer, laid back, warmer about the man playing with the closest thing to a grandbaby she'd ever have. "You still haven't told me what has brought you to Tuckers Bluff."

Nodding, Glenn sank into the nearest chair and leaned forward, his arms resting on his thighs. "I already mentioned that my daughters convinced me I was spending too much time alone in the house. Sally had been sick for a long time."

"I'm really sorry to hear that." Eileen meant it. At first, she was furious and heartbroken that Sally could take her place in such a short amount of time, but eventually she came to realize that her place was at the ranch, though she'd never expected to still be here long after the kids were grown and gone. Not till Glenn showed up on the proverbial doorstep had she paused to ponder when had she stopped planning her own future.

"Thank you. Anyhow," Glenn continued, "they began prodding me to reach out to old friends. The last couple of years we'd closed ourselves off from everyone. Then after she passed, well, seeing our friends was too hard."

Eileen nodded. She could only imagine. So much had seemed strange at the ranch without Helen. Learning to do the things Helen had always done was difficult at first in so many ways.

"Then I got a call from a local journalism student who happened to be a jazz fan. He tracked down that I still lived in the Chicago area and asked to do an interview. Talking about the old days had given me the most pleasure I'd had in years. My older daughter picked up on it and convinced me to call some of the band members. Turns out it wasn't nearly as hard as I would have thought it to be. The Internet is an amazing thing.

"First I found Bill. After only a few minutes of conversation I'd felt a little bit more alert, alive. One by one I searched the gang out and with each person I talked to I realized just how right my daughters had been. I thought I'd prepared myself for losing Sally, but all I had done was close myself off."

"So you managed to track everyone down?"

"Just about. I even made it to Florida. Scott and Johnny are still in the biz. They were working with a new singer. I even got to sit in on a couple of songs."

"Really?" Eileen felt an odd surge of something frightfully close to envy.

"I'll admit it was… nice. Not the same as when we were together, but nice."

"Like riding a bike?" she teased.

"Pretty much. When she sang 'Somewhere' I actually started to do your arrangement without even thinking."

That was one of her favorite songs to sing from West Side Story. Scott had found a way to bring in the sultry jazz rhythm and the snappy feel of the gang conflict from the original Broadway show that was irresistible to her. It had gone on the first album and gained her some fantastic reviews from the critics. "And now here you are with me."

He chuckled and leaned back. "You were a bit more challenging to locate. First I had to screw up the courage to reach out."

"That hard?" She bit back a smile. Was it wrong of her to feel a hint of satisfaction that he knew walking away when she needed him most and straight into the arms of her one-time friend was beyond a crappy thing to do?

Clearing his throat, he bobbed his head and a flash of remorse dimmed the light in his eyes. "I had expected you might have married, moved on, so when I finally began to search for you in earnest, I was looking for Callahan as a maiden name. When I couldn't track you down on any of the social media avenues and was sure you hadn't gone back to singing, I finally realized the best place to find you would be the last place you'd been."

"And here I am."

"Still taking care of little ones." His soft smile told her the words had not been said with malice.

"It does make me very happy to have little ones around again."

"You really don't miss singing at all?"

At all? That would be a lie. The first few years she couldn't even listen to music, some music, without longing to go back. Eventually that feeling went away as the sorrow of losing her dream and her sister all in the same year gave way to the joys of friends and family and small town living. Besides, she'd gotten plenty of chances to tickle her tonsils at family gatherings, especially the big fun weddings of late. But, to sing in front of an audience, to an arrangement made just for her, feel the rush, the music beating in her veins, the applause. Not till five minutes ago did she remember how much she'd loved it.

"Until today," she shook her head, "not really."

His smile spread into a sly grin. "So that means you're open to the idea."

"What idea?" Her heart hitched, skipping a beat. She wasn't sure what she wanted to hear next.

He inched forward to the edge of his seat, his eyes gleaming with anticipation. "Singing."

Singing? A funny feeling was taking root at the base of her spine and slowly crawling north. "What kind of singing?"

Eyes sparkling as bright as his smile, Glenn straightened in his seat. "Public television is doing a salute to the jazz greats. The best musicians old and new are participating. Our band, the original band, has been invited to do a reunion performance. They want us to do 'Somewhere' our way. Leeni—your way."

● ● ● ●

Scrubbing the dirt from his hands, Sean caught sight of himself in the mirror. Not that he hadn't seen himself in the mirror millions of times, but today he actually studied his reflection. Noticed the crow's feet by his eyes. The slight weathering of his skin from years of working outdoors in the sun and the heat and the wind and the rain. A few gray hairs dusted his otherwise dark hair. He chuckled to himself. Eileen had noticed them first. She called them distinguished. For at least fifteen minutes he'd sat at the kitchen table over a cup of herbal tea while she gave a near dissertation on how unfair it was that gray hairs on gentleman looked distinguished and on women they just looked old. He didn't think she had a gray hair on her head. He was pretty sure she didn't dye her hair, but he was darn sure she wasn't old.

Another thing he was pretty darn sure of, he didn't think for one minute that Glenn Baker looked at her like she was anything but the young woman he almost married. And even though Sean didn't have the right, he didn't like it one darn bit.

• • • •

Glenn splashed water in his face, blindly reaching for the sink side towel. He didn't understand what was going on. For over two decades he and Sally had a good life. Two wonderful daughters. No regrets. And yet, spending the afternoon with Eileen—chatting, babysitting— for a short while at her nephew's house today felt like his life. Comfortable, normal, what things would have been if he'd stayed the course and married Eileen. And wasn't that an unexpected concept? He'd been unsure of how she would receive the idea of a reunion performance. Hell, who was he kidding? He'd been unsure of whether or not she'd be willing to even look at him in the face without spitting in his eye. Even before the reunion offer, he'd known he needed to see Eileen again, to apologize in person for being a total jerk. Something he'd feared she wouldn't let him do when she'd not responded to his recent letter. His gut reaction to the sight of her had caught him off guard. She was still a beautiful woman, any man would have reacted the way he had. But even after that, it hadn't occurred to him that with the blink of an eye more than twenty-five years could melt away and he might want exactly what he'd wanted so long ago. Eileen Callahan.

CHAPTER SIX

Eileen sucked in a deep breath, turned the ignition off and gathering her purse and her wits, exited the car. *Reunion performance.* Ever since she'd heard those words they'd echoed in her mind like a plea for help in a vacuous cavern. Nothing else could be heard. Nearly as stunned at Glenn's declaration as she'd been to see him standing in the doorway of O'Fearadaigh's last night, she'd remained practically tongue-tied when Toni came home to take over care of the youngest Farraday girls.

For the last hour another question regurgitated in her mind over and over. Did she want to do it? *Did she?* She didn't have any better idea now than she'd had hours ago when Glenn posed the question. So much to consider. Her entire world would change. Standing in front of the ranch house she'd called home for so long another question popped into her head. Not did she want to sing again, but could she leave? *Could she?* All she knew was that Sean and Finn should be coming in from the afternoon's work any minute now and she needed to get her head out of the past and into fixing dinner.

The sound of movement in the kitchen caught her off guard. Dropping her purse on the entry table she followed the conversational sounds coming from the kitchen.

"Hi." Catherine, Connor's wife, waved one hand at Eileen over her shoulder as she shoved a container into the second fridge. "I hoped you wouldn't mind. We ran out of room in our fridge."

"Sure, but why all the extra food?"

"The compressor on the freezer went out."

"Uh oh," Eileen muttered.

"Well, it wouldn't have been such a big deal had I noticed before today. What a surprise I got when I opened the freezer this morning to pull out dinner and discovered that pretty much everything had come to a near thaw."

Eileen scanned the countertop from left to right. "That's an awful lot of meat."

"Oh, this is nothing. I've got four meatloaves, two pork chop casseroles, and a Crockpot full of sausage and peppers stuffed in the fridge waiting for the new freezer's arrival tomorrow. Y'all are now the proud owners of two roasted chickens and a king ranch casserole. I've pretty much been cooking all day. But steaks you have to eat when you grill them. Figured these'll keep in the fridge overnight and we can do a barbecue tomorrow."

"Works for me." Eileen nodded. "With only a few mouths to feed during the week, we have plenty more room in the extra freezer and fridge."

The sound of boot heels on the porch drew Eileen's attention to the back door just as Finn shoved it open. "Man, do I need a shower tonight."

Eileen smothered a smile. "No one ever said running a ranch was a clean job."

"No," Finn laughed from deep in his throat, "I don't remember anybody promising me that one."

"Where's your father?" Eileen had expected the man to come in on Finn's heels.

"We finished up a while ago. Dad came in to shower, I stayed to check one of the mares who's having some trouble with one leg. Will have to have Adam take a look at it tomorrow."

Leaning forward, Catherine gave Eileen a kiss on the cheek. "I have to run. We invited the Bradys for dinner tonight."

"Give Stacey a hug for me."

"Will do." Catherine hurried out the front door.

Had Eileen really been so self absorbed she hadn't noticed her niece-in-law's car in front? The sound of the engine started up and Eileen swallowed hard. She was definitely out of sorts.

"Looks like we're having steak for dinner." Showered and shaved, Sean walked into the kitchen, tucking his shirt into the back of his jeans.

"Baked or scalloped potatoes?" she asked on her way to the pantry, glancing over her shoulder when she didn't hear a response, surprised to see him at the sink silently staring at her.

"Baked is fine. Easier." He pulled a large platter from a side cupboard. "I'll get started seasoning these steaks."

"Catherine told you what happened?"

"Yeah, told her not to worry about them. I'd handle it as soon as I cleaned up."

Pausing to turn the oven on, Eileen dropped the sack of potatoes on the counter. "Hope everyone coming tomorrow is hungry. Want to mix up some of your—"

"Marinade." Sean nodded. "Good idea."

From the other side of the kitchen, he gathered his ingredients, setting them by the sink where Eileen washed, poked and oiled the potatoes.

"Think I'll boil up some extras and do potato salad for Sunday supper tomorrow."

"Everyone loves your potato salad." Bottle of Worcestershire sauce in hand, Sean froze mid pour. "*I* love your potato salad."

Eileen blinked and felt the tug of a smile against her cheeks. "Thanks. I'll make some extra."

"That would be nice." This time his nod was accompanied by a lazy smile that made his eyes twinkle. "So, how'd your afternoon go?"

"You mean after half the family descended en masse to spy on me? Fine." Eileen carried the tray of potatoes to the oven. Loading them in one by one, she refrained from voicing out loud the reply *different, confusing*. "I was surprised to see you in town this morning." She closed the oven door and turned on her heel, noticing his stiff stance.

"Yeah." He sighed and turned to face her. "About that."

"I should…" Their words tumbled over each other.

Submitting to a muffled chuckle, "You first," they both tried again.

Eileen walked back to the sink, turned a faucet on to fill one of the larger pots. "I shouldn't have run off this morning."

"And I should have minded my own business. It's just…" He paused and leveled his gaze with hers. "So much of what happened after Grace was born is a blur in my mind. But I remember very clearly that he made you cry."

Stripping the potato of its peel in almost therapeutic monotony,

Eileen stopped mid-motion. She had tried so hard back then to hide her feelings. Her pain. "You know, to this day I'm not sure what hurt more. Finding out I wasn't worth waiting for or finding out how easily I could be replaced."

"Maybe because you'd be wrong on both counts." He picked up the tray of marinating meat. "Your ex was a fool for not recognizing a woman like you is worth waiting forever for, and he's an idiot for not having learned you are irreplaceable." Sean turned away. "But it irks me to no end that he just waltzed back here after all these years."

Eileen returned to the rhythmic peeling of potatoes. "I'd like to think you're right. and it irked the heck out of me last night too." As far as the waltzing back into her life, she wasn't sure what to think of that. Not sure at all. So many feelings, old and new, scrambled around inside her.

"But," Sean shoved the tray into the fridge and closed the door, "not this morning?"

"I was here with you and Helen for the birth of every one of those boys. Dating Glenn didn't stop me from taking time off to be here, being engaged to him didn't stop me, and when I returned to Chicago he was always happily waiting. Never once complained about my being gone."

"But he never came with you. This morning was the first time I got a good look at the man."

"He hadn't wanted to intrude." At least, that's what he'd always said whenever she'd invite him to come along for a visit, and she'd never questioned him. Her hands stopped. Why hadn't she questioned him? Long before her sister's tragedy he should have wanted to meet her sister. Her family.

"Well," Sean broke into her thoughts, "doesn't seem to mind meeting us all now." He pulled out a knife and began chopping potatoes beside her.

"Thanks to Abbie and her fast finger texting to Jamie, the second Glenn met me at the door of the café he didn't have much of a choice."

"I'm sorry." Sean tossed the first potato into the pot of water.

"Me, too. After all these years, you deserve to know what's going on. I simply wasn't up to any questions about Glenn or why I agreed to meet him."

Sean stopped chopping the next potato and tilted his head sideways to look at her. "Because you didn't want me to know, or you didn't have an answer yourself?"

After raising a family together, she shouldn't be so surprised this man knew her that well. "Touché."

"Do you have an answer now?" He continued chopping.

"No, but at least I know why he wanted to talk to me."

Sean stifled a caustic scoff.

"He wants me to sing with the band again."

•   •   •   •

"Sing?" There were many reasons Sean would expect a red-blooded man to want to spend time with Eileen. For years he'd been baffled why more of the men in town hadn't come courting. But this, this put the hairs at the back of his neck on alert. "I see."

"For a television special." She set another potato beside him.

"Television?" Sean froze in place, the words startling him almost as much as the idea of an old flame swooping in and flying off with Eileen. Today was apparently going to be just filled with surprises. Though this last tidbit of information inched up the scale from startled to a tiny bit scared.

The appearance of Glenn Baker was enough to set any man's protective instincts on alert. Eileen was a beautiful, warmhearted, and very smart woman. Not a member of this family didn't know that and more. Her backbone, her tenacity. But only he knew her dream. The one she gave up to raise his children.

Her gaze remained steady on the potato she was peeling. "A salute to jazz artists and songwriters."

The knots slowly tightening in his stomach loosened slightly at the lack of permanence in her words. "So it's just a one time thing?"

"Maybe."

He stopped chopping and reminded himself to breathe. "Maybe?"

"Some of the original band members are still in the biz. Glenn sat in on a session with them once before tracking me down. They've been kicking around the idea of getting back together."

"And they want you?" Strangling the knife handle in a tight grip, he couldn't bring himself to move.

A grin eased across her face. "We were pretty damn good."

He couldn't argue with that. He'd heard the album they'd made. Helen would play it over and over, sometimes rocking the kids to sleep to the tunes of their Aunt Eileen. Sean was actually a little surprised none of his sons remembered that. Or perhaps they didn't know the sultry tunes came from their mama's sister. "So, that's what you want to do?"

"Might be nice. At least once." She faced him, holding the peeler up in the air. "Maybe, like talking to Glenn this morning, to find closure to the way everything ended, maybe it would be nice to see how the rest of the dream would've played out."

"I see." He swallowed the uneasiness creeping up his throat. *Her dream.* Her *gift.* What right did he have to stand in the way of that?

CHAPTER SEVEN

"I always knew Aunt Eileen could sing a mean lullaby." Finn set another plate on the table for Sunday supper. "But I had no idea."

"I don't understand what the fuss is about." Ethan followed behind Finn placing silverware. "Anytime she sang, anywhere, for any reason, people loved her."

Standing at the end of the table, Grace folded napkins. "True, but it's one thing to have a lovely voice around friends and family. Performing in front of strangers, and for a living," she clicked her tongue, "that's a whole other ballgame."

Aunt Eileen carried in a large bowl of her special potato salad. "Y'all need to quit talking about me like I'm deaf or dead. I'm right here and Ethan is correct. Y'all are making way too big a deal of all this. So I sang for a living. Big deal." But the truth was, to Eileen it *had* been a big deal. From the time she was old enough to listen to the radio with her friends, she knew she wanted to sing for a living. It was all that had mattered to her—until Grace.

"What I want to know," Finn placed the last dinner plate on the massive dining room table, "is why didn't you ever tell us?"

Smiling, Eileen shrugged one shoulder. "You didn't ask. And Finn…"

He looked up.

"We need another setting. Glenn is joining us for supper." She didn't bother to wait to register the stunned expressions, she could hear jaws snapping shut and feel eyes glued to her back. She'd have to break the other surprise on them slow and easy. Then again, what fun was that?

"You've got that swallowed-the-canary look in your eye." Sean held the second bowl of potato salad and shoved the fridge door shut with his shoulder.

"No canaries, just reminding that bunch that I'm not as old as they think."

Barely breaking his stride, the Farraday patriarch paused at her side. "Young and beautiful, nothing's changed."

"Except maybe it's time for you to hit the eye doctor," she chuckled.

One step closer to the dining room, Sean hesitated, his mouth opened, shut and then finally opened again. "My eyesight is fine." Looking away from her, he carried food into the other room, smiling at Ethan as they crossed paths.

"Need some help?" Ethan stepped fully into the kitchen.

"What?" Eileen looked up at the only light-haired son her sister had produced. Ethan was out of the military now, but still strong and handsome, and right now the narrow crease between his brows told her he was worried. No doubt about her. Especially since she stood halfway between the two rooms, empty handed, and staring at dead space where Sean Farraday had been only moments ago. "No, thank you. Just wondering if I'd forgotten anything." Like whether her brother-in-law had ever mentioned he thought she was beautiful before?

"Okay. I'll check on the meat." Ethan shifted around her, the worry lines between his brows intact.

Eileen had only a moment to consider what was up with him before Ethan's wife Allison weaved between them holding a tray of grilled corn on the cob over her head to make shimmying between them easier. "Beep beep."

Reaching up with one arm to steady the plate, Ethan slung his other arm around his wife's waist, planted a hard and fast kiss on her lips, and shot her an impish grin that promised more to come— without an audience—and whispered, "Are you okay?"

"One of these days I'm going to drop a dish right on your head and we'll both end up in the E.R." Her tone was off, overly playful, hiding something. Eileen could feel it. Then Allison blinked and barely nodded, and Eileen was sure something was up, and not in a good way.

"E.R. huh." He winked, widening that dazzling smile. "It's worth it."

"Men," Allison mumbled, but the huge grin that had replaced the hitch in her voice said she didn't seem to mind them at all. At least not this one.

Maybe Eileen was reading too much into the exchange. If anything was seriously wrong, she couldn't imagine it slipping by with a wink and a smile, even from Ethan.

Every time Eileen saw the love zinging between her nephews and their wives, it made her heart nearly melt with happiness. She couldn't help but wonder, had she beamed that way when she was with Glenn? Had he looked at her the way Ethan stood following Allison's every move, sporting a smile that made his eyes twinkle like the North Star? Could they possibly have another chance?

The chiming of the doorbell snapped her out of her musings. She'd done way too much thinking the last two days. Too much living in the past.

Escorted by no less than four of the six Farraday sons, Glenn approached cautiously with a bottle of wine. Pinot Grigio.

"You remembered." She tried hard to swallow a knot suddenly lodged in her throat.

Glenn shrugged. "Took a chance it was still your favorite."

"It is." For the first time in two days, her heart gave a little kick. A kick she hadn't felt in a very, very long time.

"Supper's almost ready." Sean strode into the kitchen. His step faltered and his smile slipped for only a moment before he moved more casually, smiled brighter. "Welcome. How do you like your steak?"

"Medium." A hint of confusion took over Glenn's face.

She couldn't blame him, this warm and friendly Sean, the man everyone loved and respected, was not the brooding silent man who had shared a booth at the cafe with them yesterday.

"Good." Sean held the welcoming smile that didn't quite reach his eyes. "I'll tell DJ. He and Connor are in charge of the grill today."

Eileen jetted her chin toward the back door, pretending this was any Sunday supper and the man she'd almost married wasn't standing at her side. "Make sure they're paying attention to the meat and not ogling their wives. Last time we left DJ and Becky in charge of the grill all the steaks came out like shoe leather."

"Yes, ma'am." Sean saluted with one hand and yanked the door open with the other.

"Would you like something to drink?" Finn came up behind Glenn.

"No, thanks, I'm fine for now."

"You sure? Aunt Eileen makes a killer lemonade or Dad keeps the fridge stocked with a selection from the new brewery in town."

"Maybe later."

Finn nodded, and scanned the counter. "Looks like all we need now are the steaks."

"Sorry we're late," Jamie called from the front door.

"Here we go." DJ came through the back door. "Take your places. Sizzling beef coming through."

Connor followed behind. "I've got the well done for the traitorous beef eaters."

"Guess it's a good thing I like medium," Glenn whispered to her.

"They'd have forgiven you," she chuckled. Maybe.

By the time the chaos of seating adults, guests, and children had passed, the next commotion of passing platters and grown brothers pretending to stab each other with forks as if they were still eight years old ensued until Sean blessed the meal.

Conversation bounced from sibling to cousin, battling with cutlery scraping the plates and quiet one on one commentaries to be heard. After each of her nephews had taken a turn peppering Glenn with questions about a musician's life on the road, the conversation turned to Aunt Eileen on the road and with a little deft distraction, Eileen managed to turn the talk back on the kids.

Glenn focused on Joanna, Finn's wife, the published author. "I'm incredibly impressed. I can hardly string two words together to form a sentence."

Joanna shook her head. "But you make beautiful music."

"I definitely play music, and how beautiful was probably in the ears of the beholder."

Just about everyone at the table chuckled at the twist on the old cliché.

"But," he continued, "I don't write any of it, just play it. You, on the other hand, weave stories that capture the mind."

"That remains to be seen," Joanna said softly.

Eileen frowned at her niece-in-law. "What do you mean? Your book on the ghost towns and Sadieville, or Three Corners as it was officially known, was a great success."

"That's only because the town has such a colorful history. I suppose it's like Glenn's music, I only played the story, I didn't create it."

"Don't underestimate yourself." Finn let his arm fall across his wife's shoulder and gently brushed his thumb along her arm. "I could have easily put this entire room to sleep retelling the same stories in a much less interesting fashion."

"Ghost towns?" Glenn asked. "Sounds fascinating."

"Right around here," Eileen put in.

"Really?"

"We have quite the history around us. Our very own Chicken Ranch," Eileen said with as much pride as if she were announcing a relationship with a renowned university and not a brothel.

Glenn's brows arched high on his forehead. "Chicken Ranch? As in the best little… whorehouse?"

"Don't look so astonished. It was, after all, a true story." Eileen held back her own laughter.

"Oh, this I've got to read about."

"I can do better than that." Before Eileen could finish her sentence, she noticed half the eyes in the room circling wide and could almost hear their jaws clicking open. "We can go *see* the old ghost town."

"Oh," Joanna almost squeaked. "Yes, Three Corners is pretty much intact. A little dirty, a little dusty, but if you like history it could be fun."

Finn shot a quick glance at DJ. "Of course, you'll want one of us to go with you. For the snakes."

"Nonsense." Eileen waved him off and faced Glenn. "Will you still be here tomorrow?"

Glenn smiled at her. "How can I pass up a real live—sort of—ghost town?"

"Then tomorrow we'll go."

"If you can wait another day," DJ said, "I can ride shotgun. You know, for the snakes."

Joanna's face scrunched up a little. "They were a bit of a problem."

"Don't be ridiculous." Eileen frowned at her nephews. "I've lived here long enough to be able to handle a little old snake."

"Or two," Joanna added.

"Or two," Eileen agreed.

Glenn nodded at his former fiancée. "Works for me."

"Then tomorrow it is." Eileen tossed a glare at her nephews across the table, almost daring them to contradict her.

Glenn smiled at her. "I think visiting the ghost town should be a hoot."

Ignoring her nephews, Eileen grinned at Glenn. So did she. *Didn't she?*

CHAPTER EIGHT

Despite the momentary difference of opinion over whether or not Eileen and Glenn needed a chaperone for a day of sightseeing, the remainder of Sunday supper had gone off without a hitch. It actually surprised Eileen how well Glenn seemed to fit in. Teasing and joking with her nephews, playing with the little ones. She couldn't help revisiting what their lives would have been like if Helen were still here.

"Now that it's just family," Ethan shifted to where his wife was putting away dishes and slid an arm around her waist, "there's been a new development that we need y'all to be aware of."

If not for the dour expressions on both their faces, Eileen would have taken wagers there was going to be a new Farraday added to the clan. Instead, she braced herself for what might have put that frown on Ethan's face.

"Please don't tell me Aunt Eileen has another man hiding in the closet?" Grace tried for a hint of humor until Sean shot his daughter a paternal glare of reproof that had her contritely easing back against her husband. "Sorry, Aunt Eileen."

"No worries," Eileen answered. Glenn had to be one heck of a surprise for everyone. "I promise to give y'all fair warning next time an old flame comes calling."

Sean nearly choked on his coffee, a couple of her nephews gaped wide-eyed, and Meg and Toni shot her a thumbs up.

Shoulders shaking from repressed laughter, Grace nodded at her aunt. "Deal."

Doing her best to smile at the teasing, Allison leaned into her husband. "I wish it were. This time it's Fancy."

That got the crowd's attention. Every person in the room stood pin straight. All sense of humor and teasing wiped away.

"What about her?" DJ asked.

Allison looked to Ethan. He nodded and squeezed her against

him. "I don't hear from her very often. When I first came to Texas some of you might remember the only news I'd received from her were in the form of two texts. *I can't do this* and later, *I've changed my mind.*"

"Right," DJ nodded. "That was when you guys decided to work together to make sure your sister didn't regain custody of Brittany."

"Yes." She stretched out her arm and grabbed hold of his free hand, squeezing it. "All I've received since is a postcard or two after her country music group had a few hits on the radio."

"They're actually pretty good," Grace added. "I bought an album."

"She does have a lovely voice." Allison smiled a moment. "This morning she called while I was in surgery." She sucked in another deep breath. "She left me a voicemail. They're performing in Dallas tonight."

"Really?" Meg said softly.

Allison blinked hard before facing the family again. "From there she'll be coming to Tuckers Bluff."

"She can't get Brittany back…" A tinge of panic laced Toni's words. "Can she?"

The moment the words were out of Toni's mouth, Eileen turned to Sean. Across the room, their eyes met and she could read the same burning concern in them that had taken hold of her heart and squeezed. *They couldn't lose Brittany.*

Grace raised her hands as if to calm all the unspoken fears and shook her head. "I wouldn't think so. Not only did she sign away her rights, she left her daughter—her infant daughter—in a box on a doorstep."

"A safe haven," DJ pointed out.

"Doesn't matter to a judge," Grace barked back. "But, that said, I don't know if she'd be entitled to some sort of visitation privileges. If her life is cleaned up—"

"She's a musician. Touring. From city to city," DJ interrupted. "Cleaned up isn't the first word that comes to mind."

"What do you think?" Brooks addressed Ethan.

"I don't know right now." Ethan's sigh came out hard and heavy. "I really don't."

"It isn't a problem until it's a problem." Sean had muttered those very words more than once through out the years. And heaven help them, she couldn't remember a single time the concern had not become a problem. Standing stiffly against the pantry wall, Sean's lips pressed tightly together.

Resisting the urge to cross the room and stand beside him proved harder than she'd expected. For years they had been a united front for the children, but starting now she might have to get used to a whole new family dynamic. And just how did she feel about that?

• • • •

"This should be fun," Rick, Tow the Line's versatile occasional keyboard player, once in a while vocalist, and mostly drummer, said from the backseat.

Fancy had no idea what about this dry Texas scenery struck the only other member of the band besides Garrett to want to tag along for this leg of the trip as having potential for fun. Behind the steering wheel, Garrett slanted a sideways glance at Fancy. She knew it was intended to be reassuring but driving past the dingy motel on the outskirts of Butler Springs only made her realize just how close she was coming to confronting her past—and hopefully her future.

Rick continued, "I mean, you read about Texas ranchers, cowboys, cattle drives, and imagine things like John Wayne and Clint Eastwood on horseback, but the closest thing to a cattle drive I've ever been to are the big statues in downtown Dallas."

"Those bronze sculptures in Dallas may be the closest you're going to come to a cattle drive. We're just visiting her sister, not taking on jobs as cowhands." Garrett was the only member of the band who knew the truth of why Fancy was so nervous about visiting her sister. Everyone else gave no thought to singing and touring and rarely taking time to go home for a visit. That was a sad but true story for so many in the music world. But only Garrett had been around on Brittany's birthday when after a glass too many of wine she'd broken down and told the best friend she'd had in forever about the little girl she'd left in Tuckers Bluff to be raised by the kindest stranger she'd ever met.

So much had changed since the day she drove that old clunker out of Tuckers Bluff, out of Texas, and nearly out of her mind.

• • • •

"Penny for your thoughts?" Sean stepped into the living room, not completely sure he wanted to know the answer to that particular question.

Eileen held out the item she'd been cradling in her hands, a photograph of Ethan and Allison the day Brittany was christened. "They're a good family."

"Yes, they are."

"I don't want to see them lose that. We can't let Allison's sister have Brittany."

"No." Sean sank into the sofa beside Eileen. "But we don't know what she wants and there's no sense fixing a problem until we know we have a problem." Setting the framed photograph on the coffee table, he glanced at the album flipped open beside it. Not an album, a scrapbook. "I haven't seen that in years."

Eileen swallowed and nodded. "I remember being so tired. Helen used to tell me that God had the good sense to not let a pregnant woman sleep through the night without waking up a few times to use the bathroom. She called it boot camp for future new moms."

"I remember." For years the mention of Helen would bring an ache so strong he thought it would never go away. Never believed that a day would come when he could smile at the memories without a trace of the pain. "I'm sorry I wasn't more help early on."

Shaking her head, Eileen waved off his apology and turned back to the album.

"I'm not sure how Helen found some of these photographs, but some nights forever long ago after I'd been pacing with Grace, when I thought I'd never be able to do right by that sweet little baby, I'd look at this album and I could hear Helen telling me 'Go for your dream. If anyone can beat the odds, it's my little sister.' And I had. I learned to tend bar, serve drinks, wait on tables, do dishes, anything that would pay the bills. Eventually the singing gigs started coming. I'd work all day, sing all night and the next day get up and do it all over again.

Then one day, all I had to do was sing all night. I'd done it. I had my dream career."

"Helen was very proud of you. We both were. You'd come a long way from that sixteen year old girl who traveled in a gaggle of teens and giggled all the time."

"You remember that?"

"Hard not to. All I had were two male cousins who lived in Austin. There were no teenage girls in my family. Let's say you and your friends made an impression."

"I suppose it could have been worse. We could have scared you off."

"Not a chance. You know how much work goes into running a ranch. I was just like Finn. Lived and breathed this place with my father. I was so annoyed he insisted I go to college." Sean paused a moment, remembering the day he'd sat across from Helen in class and knew he owed his father a debt of gratitude for being a stubborn old coot. "Anyhow, once Helen and I decided that our future was together, she wanted me to spend more time with your family. I didn't know why, but the few times we managed to visit, whether it was family dinner just for the day, or longer for the weekend, the house was always filled with giggling teenagers."

Eileen rolled her eyes. "The reason we always had a house full of girls is because every last one of my high school friends was madly in love with you and the minute I mentioned Helen was coming home with her boyfriend, the Texas cowboy, none of my friends could think of anyplace they'd rather be than my house."

"You're kidding me?"

"Nope. And to tell the truth," Eileen held up her hand and pinched her two fingers almost together, "I may have had a teensy little crush on you myself."

"Now I know you're pulling my leg."

"Maybe. Maybe not." Eileen shrugged on a soft laugh and pointed to the scrapbook. "But looking at this record of my career that Helen made, and remembering her words... How much she believed in me. I knew not only did I have to do right by Grace and the rest of you, I could almost hear Helen telling me of course I could."

"You did better than right. You were the mother my children

needed. The backbone this family needed and," he searched for the words but none seemed to be good enough, "so much more. Thank you."

Eileen stared into his eyes and Sean swore he could feel his heart pounding from the inside out. *So much more.*

CHAPTER NINE

"Your family was teasing about the snakes, right?"

Eileen briefly took her eyes off the road to look at Glenn. "No."

"I see." The expression of complete and utter horror on his face was almost laughable. "So what do we do if we, uhm, see one?"

"Shoot it." She slanted another sneak peek at her passenger and bit back a smile. Never before had she actually seen anyone turn so close to sheet white. "Don't worry. I know how to hit what I'm aiming at."

This time his eyes rounded so big and wide, for a few seconds she considered if his eyeballs really could fall out of his head. "You shoot?"

Chuckling, Eileen nodded. "Very well."

"I see." His gaze returned to the road ahead and silence hung for a few more minutes. "Not sure which makes me more nervous, a rattle snake or you with a gun. Did you bring one?"

"This is West Texas. Leaving your ranch without a gun is like driving off in a truck without gasoline."

She could feel his gaze burning into her. "What else do you know how to do? I mean, that you didn't do before?"

"Well," she blew out a breath and tipped her head in thought, "I guess the most important thing is I know how to cook and feed twenty or more people."

"That I noticed. Even though the steaks were grilled outside, I could see who was actually running the kitchen. Plus, several people oohed and aahed at the mention of your special potato salad."

"Not much to making that."

He seemed to relax a little in his seat. "Better than you used to be able to do."

"True." She chuckled a little louder remembering how often her meals had been charbroiled without a grill.

"What else?"

"I also can ride a horse and not fall off. I can assist with birthing calves and foals, even though I rarely have to. Especially with Adam in the family. He could tend to any sickly critter almost since he was out of diapers."

"I'm impressed. I'm afraid if you put me on a horse, I'd fall off the other side."

"That's been known to happen." She resisted the urge to rub her hip that had hit hard Texas dirt more times than she cared to remember. "But it's not so bad once you get the hang of it."

"And you got the hang of it?"

"I did." How long it took her not to spook at the sight of animals twice as tall as her, who rocked like a bough about to break when they walked, was a story for another time.

"And you like it?"

She cocked her head to one side, keeping one eye on the road and the other on him. "Yes. I love my life here." *My boys and Grace.* It had taken years, but she'd gotten used to the dirt and the dust and manure and hard work.

"And the music?"

Yes. What about the music? "I'd be lying if I said this opportunity didn't...intrigue me."

"I suppose intrigue is better than a flat out no."

"Did you expect me to say no?"

"You haven't said yes." He shifted in his seat, angling more in her direction. "I've been trying to read you and sometimes I think you really want to do this, and then others I think I'm reading you all wrong and you could not care less. And sometimes I'm not sure you're paying any attention at all."

She was paying attention now. Mostly. Except for the part of her mind that was clear across the county, in Tuckers Bluff, wondering was it something in the stars, some type of retrograde that was bringing all these surprise visitors to town. And would surprise visitor Fancy the singer prove to be a problem?

"Like now." Glenn straightened. "Eileen?"

The sound of her name shifted her thoughts. "Yes?"

"You're here, but your mind is somewhere else. Want to share?"

Did she? Once upon a time she would have shared anything with this man. Now, she didn't have a clue. And even if she was inclined to talk, Sean had said it best, there isn't a problem until it's a problem. So, whatever was happening in Tuckers Bluff could be handled without her. All the parties involved were legal and intelligent adults. At least Ethan and Allison were. She couldn't attest to the abilities of a woman who left her child in a box. Either way, hovering wouldn't make any difference. None of her family were young children where a kiss from Aunt Eileen or a Band-Aid could make things all better. Nope, the kids needed to solve their own problems, no matter how much she wanted to hog tie Fancy and lock her in the closet until Brittany was twenty-one.

"Eileen?" he repeated.

She blinked. Twice. "Yes. I was just thinking Ethan and the others are all grown up."

Glenn chuckled. "Looked that way to me."

Grown and married and raising families of their own. They should, and can, handle their own problems without her interference. Maybe Glenn's arrival was serendipitous. Perhaps Fancy showing up was fate working to show her that her boys didn't need her any more. That it was time to finally live her own life. To move on.

Patiently waiting in silence, Glenn watched her put her thoughts together. That had been one of the things she'd once loved about him. She could be whoever she wanted to be. Do whatever she wanted. Until staying with her sister was one thing too much. None of this ruminating was helping her make up her mind. Which life did she want to live? Only one way to find out. And visiting a ghost town was as good a place as any to start.

• • • •

"Did you sleep well?" Meg held out a tray of warm muffins.

"Yes." Fancy hoped the owner of the B&B wasn't terribly observant. The dark circles under Fancy's eyes from not one but several nights spent tossing and turning would belie the single positive response. "This is a lovely home."

Meg beamed. Her husband, Ethan's brother and Brittany's uncle, remained unreadable.

"These are fantastic," Rick mumbled around a mouth filled with blueberry muffins.

"My sister-in-law bakes them."

"Sister-in-law?" Surely it couldn't be her sister. Allison was brilliant but she'd never shown any interest in the kitchen. Besides, what surgeon baked for a bed and breakfast?

Meg nodded. "Toni is married to my husband's brother, Brooks."

Running through her memory banks from her time in Tuckers Bluff, Fancy did her best to place which of the six siblings was Brooks.

Reaching for a second muffin, Rick freely moaned with delight. "Does she have a sister?"

"Yes, but word on the street is she can't bake worth a darn."

Rick shook his head. "Too bad, it could have been true love."

Fancy, on the other hand, hadn't felt like eating. So far she'd swirled her eggs in the syrup from the French toast, but didn't think she'd actually taken a bite of breakfast. Her mind was counting down the minutes until her sister's arrival. The phone call last night to inform Allison she had reached Tuckers Bluff safe and sound had been brutal. Allison was reserved but friendly, and the few words spoken to arrange for this morning's meeting were as stilted and brittle as her mom's winter peanut crackle.

With every passing tick of the clock she'd felt less and less like consuming any food. Except now all this talk of muffins had her thinking she could manage one swallow.

"They taste even better with a little butter on them." Meg set a fresh tub on the table. Her hostess had been polite and reserved late last night when they'd checked in. A subtle shift that told Fancy loud and clear the woman had figured out who she was. "I'll admit, after Toni's mimosa cake balls, these are my favorite."

Okay, first bite and Fancy was a fan. "Maybe Neil could write a song about these."

Garrett shrugged. "If he throws in a cowboy, and a broken heart it could be a huge hit."

"And great advertising for the town." Meg laughed, the first hint of the lighthearted person who had taken their reservation and talked up her little town.

"Oh, and a dog," another guest added. "You have to toss that in!"

The room filled with more laughter as the grandmother clock in the hall clanged the hour. The easy mood Fancy had indulged in for all of two minutes slid away. With near military precision, the front door squeaked open and footsteps traveled down the hall. Garrett shot her a you-can-do-this look of confidence and she prayed more today than any day before that he was right, and that this trip would be enough to bring her what she'd always wanted.

A wall of solidarity in the form of her daughter's father holding her sister's hand came through the doorway. Fancy pushed to her feet, sliding her hands down along her denim skirt. "Hi Allison."

Her sister stood straight and strong and suddenly her lower lip trembled, her eyes sparkled with moisture and blinking fast at the water dripped down her cheeks, she softly muttered, "Fancy." A second later, her baby sister's arms were tight around her and all Fancy could think was how many years she'd foolishly wasted.

● ● ● ●

"Okay." Glenn could see the old wooden buildings at the end of the bumpy road. This wasn't a building or two on a tumbleweed-laden road. This was still an intact town. "Not what I expected."

Eileen slanted a glance in his direction. "What did you expect?"

"I don't know," he shrugged, "but not this."

That made Eileen laugh from deep in her belly and he remembered what a beautiful sound it was.

"I thought we'd park here on the edge, then we could walk to the church and back."

"Works for me." He squinted, focusing on the end of the street then slowly scanned the old wooden sidewalks. "Where are the snakes hiding?"

"Tall grass usually."

There was plenty of dirt and dust as far as he could see, but no grass. "Where?"

Eileen stretched her arm out, a slender unpolished nail pointing in the distance to the left. "From what I remember Joanna and Finn ran into trouble in the churchyard." Her eyes narrowed. "But it looks like someone may have gone at it with a weed whacker."

"Are you telling me millennial ghosts have learned to use lawn tools?"

"Oh, brother. Don't even go there." Eileen rolled her eyes. "Come on."

Slowly they walked side by side, peeking in windows, checking doorknobs. When they got to the old saloon the doors opened easily. "Here," he said.

"Oh, wow." Eileen's jaw nearly hit the floor. "This is—"

"Not what you expected?" Glenn teased.

"Someone's been having a field day with a broom and scrub brush."

Glenn sniffed the air. "Lemon cleaner too. So what we have here is a savvy and neat freak ghost."

"We do *not* have a ghost." Eileen ran her hand across the neat as a pin and shiny bar top and for a second he thought he saw her shiver.

The floors were well worn but clean. Only a few scattered tables and sundry chairs filled the large room. Most likely a fraction of the original furniture.

"This is a little creepy." Eileen brushed her arms.

Thoroughly amused at this place and her reaction, Glenn stepped in closer. "I think it's cool."

Rolling her eyes at him once more, Eileen shook her head and spun on her heel mumbling, "Men."

"Shall we explore upstairs or continue down the street?" he asked.

Eileen's gaze trailed up the wooden stairs to what back in the day would have most likely been the private…entertainment rooms. "I think I'd like to see what else is out here."

"Works for me." He held the door for her and watched the gentle sway of her hips as she walked past him. Some things really didn't change. "You know, this town reminds me a little of that town outside of Reno we played in our first year on tour."

Strolling beside him, she stopped to cup her eyes and peer into a dirty window before glancing back over her shoulder at him. "I'm not remembering anything like this."

"Well, it was more cleaned up. The sidewalks were concrete. The town was much bigger too, but a few blocks of the main street felt exactly like this. The hall we sang at was a converted saloon."

Eileen snapped straight, her eyes twinkling. "With the red curtains on the stage."

"That's the one."

"I'd completely forgotten about that." A whimsical smile took over her face. Apparently, she held fond memories of that first year together too, and that was a very good thing.

"Rumors were that the town had a resident ghost too."

"This town does *not* have a ghost." And apparently she hadn't lost any of her stubborn Irish either.

They'd walked almost to the end of the street and stopped in front of the old bordello. The house with the history that had caught Joanna's interest. The house that now had two shadows in the front window.

"And that, Miss Callahan," he smiled and waved a hand at the gabled porch, "is probably your ghosts."

CHAPTER TEN

"**H**oly Casper." Eileen stopped dead in her tracks. There is no such thing as ghosts. Absolutely no such thing. *Absolutely.*

"Shall we go look?" Glenn waved his arm along the walkway toward the front door. "Could be interesting."

"Hmm," Eileen muttered, silently repeating her mantra *there's no such thing as ghosts.* Slowly making her way up the path, out of nowhere a soft wind blew across the neatly trimmed yard. *No such thing as ghosts.* So distracted by the shadows inside, she hadn't noticed the yard till now. Someone here too had been busy with that weed whacker. A real someone. A human someone. So what if she didn't have a clue who. Or why. *No such thing as ghosts.*

"Could use a coat of paint." Glenn's soft whisper sent a shiver down Eileen's spine. When his fingers reached out and touched her arm, she jumped almost a foot forward. "Sorry," he added.

"Not a problem." She was being absolutely ridiculous. There was a perfectly logical explanation. She just wasn't all that sure she cared to know what it was. At this particular moment a nice hot cup of tea—in Tuckers Bluff—was sounding wonderful.

The front door creaked slowly open and instinctively stepping back, Eileen bumped into Glenn. His breath hitched and for the first time since he started teasing her she got the impression he was a bit concerned he might not be teasing after all.

The creak grew louder with every inch the door eased back out of the way and waving her arm behind her, Eileen finally latched onto Glenn's hand. *No such thing as ghosts.*

A tall carrot-topped slender figure appeared in the doorway only to have a short round blonde squirm to the front. *Sisters!*

Letting out a long deep breath, Eileen softly muttered, *there's no such thing as ghosts.* Maybe next time she wouldn't let her imagination run away with her.

"Well now, isn't this a nice surprise." Sissy rubbed her hands together with delight.

"Yes. Yes, it is," Sister agreed, beaming from the front door. "And who have we here?"

As if the two women and half of Tuckers Bluff didn't already know. Eileen stepped up onto the porch. "Sister and Sissy, this is an old friend, Glenn Baker."

"Nice to meet you," the two siblings echoed.

"Likewise." He bowed just slightly from the waist, sending the two women momentarily into a matched fit of giggles.

"We've been working hard for weeks," Sister said. "I hope you like it."

"Oh my." Crossing the threshold, Eileen was convinced she'd stepped back in time. "Oh my," she repeated.

"We petitioned the state to return it to us as the only heirs. Since this was our great-great-granny's home and all," Sister explained.

"Yes," Sissy added. "Approval didn't take long at all. We thought it would be fun to fix the old place up. Make it more appealing to tourists."

"That's right," Sister picked up where Sissy left off. "This way when they're done poking around here they'll come spend money in Tuckers Bluff."

Eileen blew out a whistle. "You did all of this? Just the two of you?"

"Jamison helped. After we did a little sprucing up—"

"Sprucing up?" Eileen mumbled. Even Mr. Clean would have scrubbed his fingers to the bone.

"Yes, well. Your nephew made a few repairs here and there. Might have loaned us his painting crew, though you didn't hear that from us," the taller of the two sisters whispered conspiratorially. "Then he let us have the pick of all the old furniture in the pub's attic. He and Frank helped us bring it over last Sunday afternoon."

"Frank?" Eileen asked, not really surprised that the old Marine would get involved.

The two sisters nodded. Their heads bobbed with such force it was a miracle they hadn't fallen off.

"We love how it turned out. We've been thinking it might be fun to let tourists spend the night and visit with the ghosts."

"Told ya." Glenn smiled.

"Don't." Eileen held her hand up. "We're not going there again."

"Would you like to look around?" The mismatched sisters stepped to opposite sides and urged Eileen and Glenn across the room.

"Now this," Eileen took in the room, "reminds me of that gig we did in Nevada. The rich colors, the Victorian era furniture. Remember the woman who worked the registration desk? She must have been a hundred and fifty if she was a day." Eileen smiled, wiping her hand over an antique secretary.

Glenn chuckled. "She wore those high-collared, long-sleeved, to-the-floor dresses. Anyone would think she'd stepped out of an American Gothic painting."

"That's right." Eileen spun around, grinning. "And lots of lace and the sourest expression. I teased she must be—"

"Lurch's sister." Glenn's laughter rumbled, pulling a laugh from deep inside Eileen.

The two softly began to sing, "They're creepy and they're kooky," and by the time their voices had grown stronger and Eileen belted out "neat," Sister chimed in, "sweet," and Sissy managed "petite" before all three women burst into a fit of giggles.

Almost doubled over with laughter, Glenn slid his arm around Eileen's waist. "Those were fun years."

"Yes," her cheeks ached from laughing, "they were very good years."

Sister and Sissy continued singing the theme song from the old TV show while leading the way up the stairs. Eileen couldn't get over what a wonderful job they'd done restoring the old place.

"Oh my." Just to the left of the top of the stairs, Eileen froze in front of a large framed photograph.

Sissy and Sister stopped and spun about. Both women frowning at the delay and then taking in Eileen's interest in the photograph, the sisters instantly sported matching smiles. Considering their difference in height, shape, and coloring, their smile was just about the only thing that matched.

Sister stepped in closer and pointed to the large gilded frame. "That's our great-great-grandmother Lilibeth and her sister, Siseley.

Both were mail order brides back in the day."

"Yes." Eileen nodded. "I remember that story, but when Joanna was sorting through all the photos, I don't ever remember seeing this one."

"No?" Sissy asked. "Well, it's one of our favorites."

"Those are beautiful dogs," Glenn noticed.

"Yes," Sister agreed. "Part Shepherd of some kind and part wolf. According to the diaries we found, they were from the same litter. The family stories say the dogs are the reason the two sisters found their perfect husbands. Even after our Lilibeth's sister married a miner and moved to California, the diaries said sometimes Lilibeth swore she'd still see both dogs romping about on the prairie."

"Her sister moved to California?" Eileen asked.

Sissy nodded.

"And took the dog?" A strange idea was forming in the back of her mind. One of those dogs looked an awful lot like Gray and she'd bet her last dime that if she showed the photograph to Ethan and Allison, the other dog would bear a resemblance to the San Diego matchmaker. What were the odds that offspring of these two dogs were still wandering around today? She rolled back on her heels. Interesting indeed.

"Don't you look like the cat who swallowed the canary." Glenn inched closer. "Care to share?"

"It's nothing, just nice to know some things never change."

● ● ● ●

"You look good," Fancy whispered, still hanging onto her little sister. "The famous doctor," she added.

Allison coughed out a laugh and eased from the embrace. "Says the famous singer."

There was no missing the gentle way Ethan kept a protective hand on her sister.

"Ethan," Fancy eked out in a more even tone than she would have thought possible. After all, what does one say to the man whose baby she gave up?

"Fancy," he smiled. She definitely remembered that smile. And those eyes. How had she forgotten the eyes that had told her almost instantly this was a man she could trust. And they hadn't lied. For four days he'd kept her safe and sane and though he didn't know it, helped her get her head on straight for what might have been the first time in her life.

She looked around the two. "You didn't bring her?"

Allison inched back, her hand reaching behind her and slipping easily into her husband's grasp.

"No." He cleared his throat. "We thought it best that we talk first."

Yes. Of course. Long lost sister aside, now came the part that wouldn't be easy. She turned her head and Garrett had come to stand only a foot or so behind her. "This is Garrett, the lead singer in the band."

A true southern gentleman, Garrett waited for Ethan to extend his hand. A true Texas gentleman, Ethan did just that.

"And this," she twisted around and pointed to her other band member eating breakfast, "is Rick. Best musician a group could ask for. If you need an instrument played, he's your guy."

Still shoveling food into his mouth as fast as he could, Rick gave a quick wave and returned to his meal.

Both Ethan and Allison waved back.

"Did the entire band come?" Ethan asked.

"No." Garrett shook his head. "The others have families they wanted to spend the short break with."

Meg came out of the kitchen, kissed Allison on the cheek and then her brother-in-law, tipping her head toward a couple of lingering guests in the parlor. "May I suggest y'all make yourselves at home in our apartment."

Allison's "Thank you" tumbled over Fancy's "That won't be necessary."

Meg's brows rose with surprise, then regaining her composure, she flashed a brief smile. "Well, I have some paperwork to do. If you'll excuse me."

The silence that hung for the next few moments was anything but comfortable. Fancy had so many things she wanted to say, questions she wanted to ask. Too many years had passed. She didn't know where to begin.

"Fancy talks about you all the time," Garrett started, once he'd realized no one else was going to speak first. "I especially like the story about the dog and your aunt's favorite scarf."

Allison almost choked on her own spit. "You remember that?"

"Every minute of it." Fancy smiled. "I thought you'd done a wonderful job of bandaging his paw. The colors matched Champ's fur beautifully."

"Too bad Aunt Millicent didn't agree with you."

"Every future doctor has to practice first aid on a patient somewhere. You picked a very loveable—"

"And very patient," Allison added.

"Yes, and very patient," Fancy concurred, "Golden Retriever to work on."

Another guest came down the stairs and made her way into the kitchen, politely smiling at the people huddling in the middle of the room. Maybe they *should* use Meg's apartment. They needed to talk, the sooner the better, and in private made the most sense.

Garrett inched a fraction closer, his hand hovering above her shoulder as though he were ready to knock someone clear across the room if they so much as threatened to invade her private space. Friend and protector, thank heaven for someone in her corner. "Is there a little coffee shop around here? Someplace we can talk in private?"

"Yes." Fancy nodded. "I really don't want to displace Meg or her routine."

"The café around here is busier than a salmon swimming up stream," Ethan's calm expression remained unchanged, "but the pub doesn't serve lunch. At least not to the general public. It's a short walk if you don't have any objections?" He let his words linger.

"Did someone say pub?" Rick swallowed his last bite quickly and appeared on Fancy's other side.

Garrett rolled his eyes. "It's only ten o'clock in the morning."

"As the saying goes, it's five o'clock somewhere."

Ethan slid his phone from his pocket. "Well then, if we're all in agreement, I'll just give Jamie a call. The man spends most of his day in the office doing whatever it is pub owners do at a desk."

The last to step outside, Rick looked up and down Main Street.

"As far as sleepy little towns go, this one is pretty cool."

"We think so." Allison walked in step by her husband.

It still rattled Fancy's senses that her sister had wound up with Brittany's father. It also made her heart swell. She'd loved her kid sister more than anything in the world. That had been one of the reasons Fancy had kept her distance and the nickname bestowed upon her. Allison had so much potential and Fancy feared her influence could only hold her kid sister back. Knowing in the end her sister wound up with the world's most perfect man, in the most perfect place, meant everything to her. More than she would have thought a few days ago. As a matter of fact, nothing felt the same as it had a few days ago.

From behind large paned glass windows, store owners waved at Ethan and Allison as they passed by. Comments like "Lovely day for a walk" or "Nice to see you in town" could be heard from the other side of a few open doors.

They strolled past the police station and a snake of recollection slithered to the forefront of her mind. Leaving Brittany behind may have been the best thing she could have done for the baby girl at the time, but it had been the hardest damn day of Fancy's life. She'd had no idea how much any one person could love another tiny human being. All she'd ever wanted for her little girl was to have the best life could offer, and at the time, that wasn't with Fancy.

"Here we are." Ethan waved an arm at the massive dark wood door.

"Oh." Fancy glanced up at the sign. "This is new."

Two deep furrows slid between his brows. "Yes, my cousin opened it recently with a little help from some of the family."

"O'Fearadaigh's," she said softly.

Still frowning, Ethan held the door for everyone to pass through. "That's the original spelling of the Farraday name back in Ireland."

"Of course it is." Fancy sighed. The perfect man. The perfect town. The perfect family. What was she thinking coming back for her little girl?

CHAPTER ELEVEN

S o what if after loading the truck, Eileen and Glenn had run off and climbed in like a couple of teens on a first unchaperoned date? Sean Farraday swung the sledge hammer onto the post.

Seeing his former sister-in-law happy was a good thing. *Former?* Once more he hammered the new fence post a little deeper into the hard Texas ground. He'd taken a vow till death do us part. Was there a statute of limitations on familial relations? Swinging the heavy hammer around and up into the air, he brought it crashing down one more time and froze, staring at the new section of fencing. *Former. Death do us part.* Did the in-law relation die with the spouse? In more than twenty-five years since he'd lost Helen, since the vows had played out, not once had he stopped to consider what that made Eileen to him. Definitely Aunt Eileen to the kids. Always Helen's sister. But to him?

From his breast pocket, the loud trill of a call echoed in the crisp West Texas air. He and Finn were supposed to work this fence line together but reports of mountain lions near one of the back pastures had him and the ranch foreman, Sam, riding the line for any signs of trouble. The kid was probably checking up on his old man. Seeing if he remembered how to repair a fence. *Kid.* That made him laugh. Finn was a married man. Every one of Sean's children were all grown up and a few raising families of their own now. Finn probably wouldn't be too far behind on that count. While there was no talk of babies, Sean recognized the look in Joanna's eyes every time she got close to one of his grandbabies. Yep, it wouldn't be long now. "I still have all ten of my fingers," he laughed into the phone.

"Good to know." The voice belonged to Ethan, not Finn. "Are you at a point where you can stop and do us a favor?"

Even if he wasn't, unless it was something absurd like a craving for a root beer float, nothing was more important than being there for his children. Never had been, never would be. "Whatcha need?"

"Toni took the girls over to Connor's for the new toddler and horses program and can't leave. Could you bring Brittany to the pub?"

"The pub? Don't you think she's a little young to be learning the joys of a good ale?"

Ethan's voice lowered. "Fancy is here. We've agreed she can see Brittany."

"Oh." Sean swallowed hard. Though little was said, last night every one of the family had been on proverbial pins and needles considering why Brittany's birth mother would be returning to Tuckers Bluff now. Though deep down, they all knew the answer they didn't want to face.

"For now, we don't want her at the ranch."

"Of course." Not that Sean understood what difference it would make, but his son was a grown man married to a smart woman. If this was what they wanted… "I'll be on my way as soon as I wash up a bit."

"Thanks, Dad."

The call disconnected and Sean looked over the rolling land that had been referred to as Farraday country since the days his grandparents first settled the area. Ethan and Allison rented a small house not far from Brooks and Toni, one of the reasons Toni took care of Brittany with her own when Allison was working. Plans were in the making for Ethan and Allison to build on a nice piece of land close to the new hospital. Plans for their family. He prayed this Fancy wasn't going to cause any trouble. For some time now he'd had a picture in his head with all of his kids and grandkids living near or on Farraday land. He didn't want some woman swooping in and tearing apart his son's life. He liked the picture in his head just fine. His children happy and settled, him and Eileen manning the homestead to keep the family together. *Him and Eileen*?

• • • •

"Those two are a hoot." Glenn slid out of the passenger side of the ranch pickup.

"You could have knocked me over with a feather when they opened that door." Eileen slammed the door and scooted around to the back, not mentioning that the touch of his hand had almost sent her flying into the next county. Talk about letting her imagination run away with her.

"This place looks different in daylight." Glenn came around to meet Eileen, glancing sideways at the pub windows.

"You're timing was perfect. You arrived on opening night." Eileen popped the lids off the two ice chests and reached inside, handing off a foil covered tray. "Might as well make yourself useful."

"No problem, Miss Kitty," he teased.

"You know…" Eileen couldn't decide if she found Glenn's play on Miss Kitty and Marshall Dillon amusing or ridiculous. Though somewhere deep down she was eating up the flattering attention. "You really need to get out more."

Glenn chuckled softly. "What are these for?"

"I promised Jamie a couple trays of my rice pudding."

"Your rice pudding?" He balanced the tray on one hand and opened the pub door with the other.

"Don't look so shocked. I told you I learned to cook for twenty or more people. This was my mother's recipe. My sister Helen tweaked it a bit and after all these years the whole town knows it's the best. Now any one dining here from out of town will know too." Eileen stuttered to a halt at the people seated inside. She'd expected to have to hunt Jamie down in the back. "Oh, hi."

Glenn's attention went straight to the man tinkering at the piano in the corner.

Most folks were huddled around one table. Jamie was behind the bar shining brass fixtures. Immediately Eileen's heart caught in her throat. The strawberry blonde woman she'd never met before had to be Allison's sister, Francine—Fancy.

"Let me help you with that." Ethan sprang from his seat and arrived at her side in a flash, removing the large tray from her hands.

Angling her head and lowering her voice, Eileen whispered, "Is everything all right?"

"So far," he whispered back.

"I've got this." Jamie relieved Glenn of the tray. "Thanks."

Handing the tray over and following the pub owner, Glenn glanced at the man and the piano. "Looks like an oldie."

"Yeah. It was in the back. I was shocked that it played as well as it did. Had a piano restorer come in from Butler Springs and he was just as surprised it wasn't in worse shape."

"Mind if I take a closer look?"

"Suit yourself," Jamie called over his shoulder.

The moment the piano man stopped tinkering, Glenn ran his finger along a few of the keys. "These are ivory."

The man seated pushed back and stuck out his hand. "Rick Mason. Want to give it a whirl?"

The way Glenn eased onto the bench anyone would think he hadn't seen a piano in years. Eileen suspected that one session with the band was on a keyboard not a piano. Both made music, but even she knew there was something different about playing an honest to goodness piano. His fingers curled over the keys and beautiful sounds seeped across the nearly empty pub.

"Wow," Ethan mumbled beside Eileen.

A smile tugged at the corners of her lips. She'd actually forgotten how well he could make music out of just about any instrument. The rambling of notes flowed into a very specific tune. One she remembered so well. Her fingers began to snap with the rhythm of the music and her feet brought her closer to the piano. She could feel every note from her fingertips to her toes. Lord how she'd missed this.

● ● ● ●

Parked in front of the pub, Sean hurried around to the passenger side of the truck to unstrap Brittany from the car seat. For decades ranch kids had ridden in the backseat, front seat, bed, heck, a time or too he'd been known—a lot older than Brittany of course—to ride on the hood, and they'd all survived. But the law was the law, not to mention the thing came in awfully handy with only him and a toddler. He never was one of those parents who rode with a kid in his lap. That just struck him as foolhardy and a miserable heartbreaking accident waiting to happen. So, every single truck at the ranch had a car seat just in case immediate transport was needed. Like today.

Holding a grinning blonde-haired cherub in one arm, he kicked the truck door shut. From inside he could hear traces of a familiar tune played on a piano. The moment he opened the door he recognized the song, and the voice. Eileen stood, eyes closed, her arms open wide, belting out with more power than he remembered hearing in a very long time. He stood frozen, afraid to move, to make a sound, to break the spell. She was in the zone. The piano was with her for every note, and the energy in the room was palpable.

Her fingers spread, one arm lifted and she sang, "Cloudy or Sunny" and sent goose bumps up his arms, and most likely the arms of every person in the place. She was on fire. The piano vibrated, her arms rose high and the last words, the title of the old popular tune "Come Rain or Come Shine" ricocheted around the room. Her arms fell to her side, applause from the handful of occupants filled the space and Eileen opened her eyes. She looked… stunning. Had Sean ever seen her this happy?

For a few seconds she seemed startled and then a smile slid across her face, her eyes twinkled and his heart dropped. They were going to lose her. He could feel it in his bones.

"That was amazing." A blonde woman Sean had never met who must be Allison's sister was the last one still applauding.

"Wow." Jamie had practically flown over the bar to give his aunt a hug. "I've heard you and Mom sing together enough to know you could carry a mean tune but, wow, I'd never heard anything like that."

Behind her Glenn had pushed away from the piano and come to his feet. Standing over her he nodded. "You haven't lost your touch."

Brittany made a loud gleeful noise and began clapping again. All heads turned to her, the smiles and praises over Eileen's impromptu performance forgotten for the family business at hand. Immediately, Allison jumped to her feet and scurried across the small space to retrieve the beautiful little girl. "Mama," Brittany cooed, throwing herself at the woman who had been the only mother she'd known since she'd been left on a doorstep.

"How's my girl?" With the reluctant stride of a person taking their final steps, Allison eased toward her sister.

"She calls you Mama?" Fancy asked on a shaky whisper.

Allison nodded. "We tried Auntie but somehow she seemed to connect that if Toni is Mama to Helen, and Catherine is Mama to

Stacey, then I had to be—"

"Mama," Fancy finished for her.

Ethan fell into step beside his wife and Brittany threw her arms up. "Da."

Kissing his wife on the temple, Ethan pulled his little girl toward him and twirled her overhead, receiving heartfelt giggles before he took a seat at the table. Brittany's sweet smile slipped. Pressing her head against her father's shoulder, she studied the new people staring quietly at her.

Halfway between the door and the table, instinct told Sean to stick around. This was a time when the family might need to circle the wagons. Without hesitating, he started toward the tiny stage where Eileen stood watching the interaction with the same eagle-eye intensity he had. The moment his gaze saw Glenn inch closer to her, Sean recognized the move. A protective gesture that stopped Sean mid-step. Air sucked from his lungs. She deserved a real man to protect her. One who appreciated her. He pivoted around and strode to the bar.

"Isn't this something," Jamie whispered, wiping the same spot on the bar.

Sean nodded. "What did I miss?"

"Well, I've been a bit far back to hear it all. But seems like she wants to get to know her daughter."

The words made Sean cringe. Normally he didn't judge people on hearsay, but this woman had done the unforgiveable.

"That can't be good," he mumbled.

"Like I said, hard to hear everything but there was lots of crying and hugging going on for a while. I think the sisters are bonding."

"Bonding, huh?" Sean blew out a sigh. "Who's the guy with her?"

Jamie shrugged. "Don't know."

"It's his band she sings in." Eileen slid onto the stool beside him. "That's all?"

Eileen turned her head to the small group of four around the table, five with Brittany. "Not sure yet."

A soft mellow tune came from the piano where another man and Glenn were tinkering and talking. "And the other fellow?"

"Another member of the band."

Sean nodded. "What's your take on this?"

Her eyes narrowed. "Something's not lining up."

"What do you mean?"

"She's not what I expected. Her tone of voice, her eyes, the few things she's said. Doesn't sound like a woman who would drop a helpless baby on a doorstep."

Sean studied the woman in question. One thing he'd learned to trust all these years was Eileen's instincts. The woman had a sixth sense that could get her and anyone else in or out of trouble, but she usually hit the nail on the head. He'd come to rely on that instinct more than once raising seven kids alone. No, not alone. At least not yet. His mind turned over the idea of playing Grandpa without Eileen. Of Sunday suppers without Eileen. Of morning coffee without Eileen. Bedtime tea without Eileen. The rest of his life just took an unexpected, and unwanted, left turn.

CHAPTER TWELVE

For the first time in her life Fancy understood the expression heart-stopping. This little girl, her little girl, was so much more than beautiful.

"She looks like you." Fancy glanced at Ethan for only a minute before returning her attention to the toddling cherub.

Ethan ducked his chin and placed a feather-light kiss atop Brittany's head.

"Hi, Peanut." Speaking softly, Fancy curled and uncurled her fingers in a more entertaining wave hello. "I brought you something."

Brittany's eyes widened with interest. Her father's, on the other hand, narrowed with concern. Somewhere deep down, Fancy knew she would have to win over everyone's trust if she was going to accomplish what she wanted. What she thought she wanted. Just now when so many feelings bubbled to the surface at the sight of her sister, her daughter, and the family bond held by the three, Fancy realized how much she had underestimated. The look on father and daughter's faces made that perfectly clear. Allison looked totally torn, but somehow, eventually, Fancy would show them she'd changed. She simply had to.

From the bag beside her Fancy retrieved a small fluffy lamb. "I understand this little guy from a TV show is popular with kids."

Brittany reached forward, poked one finger at the stuffed toy and then giggled before clutching it tightly to her chest.

She liked it. Her little girl liked the present. Garrett barely set a reassuring hand on hers, smiled, and quickly let go. Always a support. He'd spent the hour or longer with her in the store, walking the aisles, asking questions of the sales staff and the moms shopping and finally going with the suggestion of one little girl. Well, as much of a suggestion as a two and half year old could make when she grinned at the two stuffed animals Fancy had shown her mother and grabbing at the white one yelled, "Lambie!" Once the mother had explained that her "Lambie" was at home waiting for her, Fancy had her present for her daughter. At least one of them.

"What do you say?" Allison coaxed.

Brittany managed to grin even wider, kick her feet and bounce on her dad's lap. "Tank chu."

"You're welcome," Fancy responded. The two little almost-words swelled her heart. "She seems very happy."

"She is." Ethan's words came out low and firm.

Fancy nodded. She hadn't meant to upset him, she'd only meant… "I knew she would be. I just knew it."

"Oh, Fancy." Allison bit on her lower lip and blinked back the water pooling in her eyes. The censure said everything her words did not—how could you?

"I didn't have a choice." She answered the unspoken question.

Garrett shook his head and lowered his voice, gesturing to her daughter with his chin. "This isn't the time."

No. Not with Brittany sitting on her daddy's lap. All morning she and Allison shared memory after memory of the good times, the sad times, Aunt Millicent and the hundred reasons Fancy ran away. They caught up on all of Allison's adventures and the entire time Ethan kept a hand on his wife in silent support. They'd hugged, they'd cried, they'd laughed, but the only mention of Brittany came when Fancy asked to please see her. Now she'd have to wait for another time, another chance to convince her sister and her daughter's father that she could be a good thing for Brittany.

"Excuse us." Eileen stepped up to the table. "I need to get Glenn back to the ranch. He left his car there and has to be in his hotel room for a video conference in a couple of hours."

"That makes two of us." Ethan's father stopped beside the aunt with the golden voice.

"Or," Glenn turned away from the table, "join me for dinner?"

Ethan's aunt blinked and his father clenched his teeth, making his jaw muscles twitch ever slightly.

"We can stay in town, do the video conference, go out for a nice dinner and then head back to the ranch for my car."

"If by nice you mean something more upscale than a pub or café," Ethan interrupted, "you're out of luck."

"I did have something a little more…private in mind."

"That would be the Lake House. It's a steakhouse at the edge of town in Butler Springs." Allison smiled. "They have a nice little dance floor too."

"You up for a ride to…" He looked at Allison again.

"Butler Springs," she provided.

"Butler Springs?" Glenn finished.

The aunt's face bloomed, the smile on Glenn's face rivaled that of Ethan's aunt, and Allison seemed to be quite pleased with the prospect. On the other hand, Ethan seemed to be teetering between giving his blessing and throwing the first punch. Remembering the fire in Ethan's eyes the night he'd rescued her from that drunken sailor, Fancy hoped for this guy's sake that Ethan went for minding his own business.

At the moment the aunt bobbed her head yes, the senior Mr. Farraday's gaze took on the same look Fancy had seen in his son what felt like eons ago. When it came to picking men for herself, she'd always had lousy judgment. Not even when she'd stumbled onto an outstanding specimen like Ethan Farraday had she had the good sense to latch on for dear life. But she was darn good at that outside the glass looking in thing, and something was going on here that had nothing to do with the loving tight knit family Ethan spoke of for days in San Diego. Nope, something very interesting was simmering around here and she hoped she'd get to stick around long enough to figure out who was going to win.

● ● ● ●

How could he have forgotten? Sean gripped the steering wheel and peered into the distance. The flat, gray distance. Eileen had been singing at family gatherings and murmuring the occasional soft tune while puttering in the kitchen or some other household project. She'd sung lullabies to all the children, even before Grace. But none of that was the same as Eileen Callahan on stage with nothing more than a four-piece jazz band to back her up. He and Helen had gotten Anne and Brian to babysit the kids while the two of them snuck off for a weekend in Albuquerque to watch Eileen perform. It was early on, before Glenn's group, and she hadn't quite perfected her style, but the voice, the voice was there. Here. And why did seeing her belt out the end of that tune make his chest feel as though a bull calf were sitting on it.

And now what? Doe eyes last night, ghost town frolicking this morning, and dinner tonight. Just how long was this guy going to stay? And how long before he talked Eileen into going with him when he left?

And Brittany. What the heck was going on at the pub? As sure as he knew his name was Sean Patrick Farraday, son of Patrick Aloysius and Sara Maureen Brookstone Farraday, he knew his son would not give up his little girl without a fight.

Thoughts rattled around his head. Too many to wrestle into submission. By the time he'd pulled in front of the ranch house his mind was as cluttered with questions and concerns as it had been before the otherwise peaceful hour-long drive.

The lights were out, only silence greeted him as he crossed into the house. For so long this house had been filled with noise, and clatter, and laughter and love. He could still feel the love and warmth, but the silence, that was something he would have to get used to.

"Don't you look like someone stole your best friend." Finn came out from the newly fashioned suite off the kitchen. Freshly showered, clean shaven and dressed for a night out.

"You and Joanna going somewhere on a weeknight?"

"Yep." Finn grinned from ear to ear. "Taking advantage of the pub being open every night for the grand opening week. Do a little boot scootin' with my wife and get some of Aunt Eileen's rice pudding."

"Let's hope more folks from around here are thinking the same thing. From the turn out on opening night, I'd guess Jamie was right on the money about how well the pub is going to do."

"None of us doubted him." Finn tucked his shirttail into his jeans. "You and Aunt Eileen should join us."

Under normal circumstances he'd have enjoyed taking Finn up on the invitation, but tonight wasn't normal. Or maybe tonight would be the beginning of the new normal—him rattling around after work in this big old house all alone with no one to talk to but the walls.

Maybe he could learn to like watching reality TV.

Finn ducked his head, narrowed his gaze, and took a step toward his father. "Is something wrong, Dad?"

No. Yes. Maybe. "No. You and Joanna go have a good time."

"She's coming in from an afternoon photo shoot with the sisters at the ghost town. They have a huge tourist plan in the making. I'm meeting her at the pub." Finn took another step closer. "Dad, you're not telling me something."

Sean shook his head. This was just the cycle of life. That's all. Nothing stayed the same forever. Hadn't he learned that lesson the hard way?

"Dad," Finn got right in his father's face, "you are scaring me. I've never seen that look on you before. What's happened? Is someone hurt?" Finn looked over Sean's shoulder to the empty living room and then back to the empty stove, his eyes widening. "Is it Aunt Eileen? Did something happen to her? Did that man—" An increasing hint of panic punctuated every word.

"No. Nothing like that." Sean glanced around the empty kitchen. Memories of Eileen trying desperately to cook for the family and ranch hands. The pitiful look of frustration and determination as she stood covered in flour, carefully following Helen's biscuit recipe. The first attempts had made it straight to the trash can. Eventually they'd gotten more and more tasty until one day he'd come home and there wasn't a lick of flour anywhere in the kitchen. Eileen held out a dish of warm biscuits, grinned from ear to ear and calmly declared, *"I think I've got the hang of it."*

"Nothing like what?" Concern remained etched on Finn's face

"Tonight your aunt is on a…" the words stuck in his mouth, "date."

Finn nodded but didn't say anything. Taking a few steps in retreat, he leaned against the kitchen counter, waiting.

Not sure what else to say, Sean turned to the fridge and pulled out a covered dish, then put it back. He wasn't really hungry anymore. Same thing with the beer, he'd held it in his hand reading the label as though he'd never seen it before and set it back in the fridge. Maybe tonight would be a good night to go to sleep with the sun.

Finn crossed his ankles and cleared his throat. "I'm guessing I wouldn't be far off the mark if I said that idea isn't sitting well with you?"

"It's not the what, it's the who." Sean ran his hand roughly across the back of his neck. "He doesn't deserve her."

"I see."

"Do you?" He took the lid off the cookie jar and pulled out a couple of oatmeal raisin cookies. Not that he was hungry or craving sweets, holding onto it and chewing gave him something to do.

"Yes. I think I do, but I'm wondering if you do."

Sean offered his youngest son, the wise old sage in a youthful body since the day he was born, a cookie.

Shaking his head, Finn asked another question. "Is this ex of hers the problem, or is no one good enough for her?"

"You've been thinking too hard. This guy didn't give her the respect she deserved. How could he have expected her to choose between a helpless baby and him? All she'd asked for was more time. It's not like they had one foot in the grave and one on a banana peel. Time was on their side."

"She had postponed the wedding more than once."

"Things happen that are out of our control."

"Maybe he thought she didn't really love him."

"Hogwash. She cried for weeks after he hung up on her refusing to push the date back again."

"Weeks?" Finn raised a brow. "Doesn't seem like all that much sulking for losing the love of her life."

"He wasn't the love of her life." Sean spun around, reaching for another cookie. Or maybe the guy had changed, maybe Glenn could be that special someone, and maybe he should have that beer after all.

"Then I'm not seeing the problem."

"The problem is…." Sean stopped and stared at his son. Eyes twinkling with delight, the kid was almost smiling. "This isn't a laughing matter."

"No." He swallowed the grin threatening to take over his face. "But I wondered what it would take to open your eyes."

"Open my eyes? You're talking in riddles."

"No, it's really quite simple and quite clear. At least it has been to most of us the last few years."

"Again, more riddles."

"Dad." He spoke as though he were about to explain rocket science to a four year old. "For over twenty years you've been married to Aunt Eileen in every sense except for a shared bedroom."

"We never—"

Finn held his hand up. "I know that. We all know that. But that doesn't change the facts. You have relied on each other for support through thick and thin, through pain and sorrow, through chicken pox and mono, through hard times and good times, basically in sickness and in health, and before today you both probably believed until death do you part."

"You're crazy. I've always known some day the right man for your aunt would come along. By the time Grace reached high school I was surprised that someone hadn't come yet."

"Why would they? She didn't need a husband's companionship. She's always had you."

He whirled around and practically shouted, "She does not have me."

"Dad." Finn pushed to his feet. "You can argue with any one of us from now till the second coming, but it won't change reality. I think you've been in love with Aunt Eileen for so long you don't remember a time you weren't." Sean opened his mouth to protest and Finn shot up his hand. "I'm not looking for an argument or cross examination. All I'm saying is if it bothers you so much that this guy is making nice with Aunt Eileen, then maybe it's time you did something about it."

Stunned, Sean stood silently staring at Finn's back crossing the house and making his way out the front door.

The kid had lost his mind. And if all his children agreed with Finn then they were all stark raving lunatics. Weren't they?

CHAPTER THIRTEEN

Layers of black clouds appeared out of nowhere. This wouldn't be the first or last time a storm brewed unexpectedly. Whether it would pass them by or release its liquid fury was yet to be seen.

The conversation in the pub had moved back to Adam and Meg's. Rick stayed talking beer with Jamie and doing his version of sampling and tasting. Sean had taken Brittany back to Connor's, and Garrett came with Fancy. In the corner of the living room, the TV was tuned to a channel with swirling colors of orange and red across the screen. "Oh, that doesn't look good," Eileen muttered.

Ethan shook his head. "Seems to be moving right past us and up to Butler Springs."

"There's a tornado watch until 8pm for the entire county." Wiping her hand on a dishrag, Meg entered the room. "Adam's cancelling appointments for anyone who doesn't live in town."

Eileen looked at the screen and turned to Glenn. "We should probably postpone tonight. Storms can get pretty nasty here and that one's heading straight for our dinner plans."

"Seems to be moving pretty quickly too," he agreed.

"Rain check?" She smiled up at him.

"Let me see if I can move the video conference to a later time and we'll head back to the ranch."

Eileen shook her head. "That will put you driving back in the thick of it and on these lonely roads that's never a good idea."

"I don't think driving back to the ranch is a great idea now either." Meg pointed at the screen.

"She's right." Ethan shrugged. "That thing could pick up speed or shift direction."

Eileen stared at the screen a moment. "It hasn't even started to rain here and the storm is coming from other side of Tuckers Bluff. I should make it home no problem."

"I don't—" Ethan started.

"Ethan Patrick Farraday, I have been driving these West Texas roads for as long as you've been talking. I'll be fine in that big old truck. I don't want to waste time jawing with you. I need to get on the road."

The way Ethan bit down on his back teeth she knew he wasn't happy about it, but she also knew that he wouldn't argue any more. She turned to say goodbye and spotted Garrett, his gaze skipping from the screen back to his lead singer. The way the man looked at Fancy made Eileen's mind wander once again to a long time ago. Had Glenn looked at her that way?

"If you're going to go," Ethan interrupted her thoughts, "you'd better go *now*. And call when you get home."

"Aye aye, Captain." She refrained from saluting. Ethan only rolled his eyes. She wished she could stick around for the conversation that had to be had over Brittany, but a bigger part of her needed to be home. Turning, she waved good bye to everyone, paused to smile at Glenn. "Call when you're done with your video conference and we'll arrange to get your car back to you."

Lips pressed tightly together, Glenn glanced out the living room window and back before nodding. "Stay safe."

Not the first time in the last few days a man had said that to her. "Will do." And with that she hurried out to the truck.

The clouds were growing darker and she needed to boogie. Concerns about lightning and hail and power outages and generators scrambled around with music arrangements, singing, cancelled weddings, and resurging dreams. The dreams were what got her. Singing—no—performing. This wasn't the same as singing along at the supermarket or at a family wedding. She couldn't deny it and now all she could think about was how much she wanted it. To give it another try.

A flash of lightning jagged across the sky and brought new thoughts to mind. Was singing all she wanted? She'd had fun today with Glenn. Even though the sisters had almost scared the bejeesus out of her, having Glenn at her back had been... nice. The wall from so many years of anger and hurt cracked enough for long forgotten memories of happier times to resurface. She and Glenn had made a good pair.

At the mouth of the driveway a boom rattled the windows moments before another flash of light brightened the inside of the truck. Definitely too close for comfort. Pulling up to the side of the ranch house, she grabbed her purse and darted to the front porch seconds before pellets of rainwater hammered down. Another minute and she would have had her second shower of the day. Stomping the dust off her boots on the porch, Eileen listened to the sound of the rain bouncing off the roof and music. Music?

For a split second she hesitated turning the knob. Were Finn and Joanna having a private evening? She retraced her steps, peering around the edge of the house in search of her nephew's truck. Gone. So was Joanna's car, but the other ranch truck was in its usual place. Sean never played music.

Turning back, she listened more carefully. The occasional downpour drowning out the melodies on the other side of the wall. Slowly turning the knob, she pushed the door open far enough to hear the familiar tune—and voice. Her voice.

• • • •

"You've been in love with Aunt Eileen."

For nearly twenty minutes after Finn walked out the door, Sean argued with an empty room. His son had lost his mind. Of course Sean understood Eileen, respected Eileen, appreciated Eileen, and yes, even loved her. He also loved the kids' Aunt Anne but that didn't mean he was in love with either of them.

"Shared everything but a bedroom."

If his son had been a few feet closer Sean would have washed Finn's mouth out with soap. She didn't deserve such a comment. Eileen had given up everything for him and the children. She was good, and honest, and loving, and caring, and smart, and beautiful, and yes, she was sexy as hell, but that didn't mean…*Sexy as hell*?

Right about when those words ricocheted in his mind like a pinball on steroids was when Sean dug out the old album that Helen had played so often. He'd listened to the entire first side of the LP and the first song on the flip side had just begun to play. Images of Eileen in the pub—her eyes closed, her voice the perfect instrument for the sultry jazz tune—swayed with the rhythms from the overhead speakers. *In love*. His son had to be wrong. He couldn't lose another woman in his life. Letting his sister-in-law go was one thing, but losing a life partner... Finn had to be wrong.

"Maybe it's time you did something about it."

Sean sucked in a ragged breath. When had things changed? How long ago had he stopped thinking of Eileen as his wife's sister? He had to face the truth, so long ago he didn't have a clue when it happened. But *in love*?

The front door pushed open and Sean stood from his seat, hurrying to turn off the music before one of his sons recognized the voice and used it to further make Finn's point. Slowing his pace, his eyes drifted closed. *"I think the man doth protest too much."* Had he really heard Helen's voice laughing at his sudden sense of panic?

"I didn't know you still had this record." Eileen inched her way to the stereo and smiled. "Not bad."

"Better than not bad. Much better." He took in the sweet expression on her face as she listened to her own voice crooning "Summertime." Gorgeous didn't begin to describe her. No wonder Glenn was back. "I thought you were going out to dinner?"

"Storm's coming in. Didn't think it safe to drive all the way to Butler Springs."

"You could have stayed in town." He refrained from saying *should have*, at least if he wanted to keep her from handing him his head on a silver platter.

She shrugged a lazy shoulder. "I like to be home in case of anything."

"Anything?" How much longer would she think of this as home? Her home.

"You know," she lifted her chin toward the gas lanterns on the shelf, "power outages, roof leaks, whatever." Thunder cracked overhead and she shuddered before taking a step closer to the shelves. "We might be needing these tonight."

As if proving her point, thunder struck again and he nodded. "Good thing the generators are ready to go."

Stretching his arm forward, his hand brushed against hers and for the first time ever, he'd have sworn the static electricity in the room was off the charts. By the way Eileen's hand jerked away and her gaze leveled with his, he'd have sworn in court that she felt it too.

On an awkward huff, he took a step back and regrouped. He was letting his imagination run away with him. The power of suggestion, Finn's suggestion, was getting the better of him. He set the gas lamp on the center of the coffee table.

Eileen set the other across the room on the side table by the stereo. "I'll fix us something to eat."

Sean nodded and followed her into the kitchen. Not that he could eat a bite, his head and his heart were completely off balance. Throughout the next song they moved side by side. Sean chopped cucumbers for a salad, Eileen transferred a small casserole from the fridge to the oven. The table was set and drinks were poured.

One song faded away and the silken sounds of "Somewhere" broke the silence.

"Maybe it's time you did something."

Turning to face Eileen, he reminded himself anything worth fighting for was worth taking a risk. Extending one hand out in front of her, he cleared his throat. "May I have this dance?"

Eileen blinked once and then again, and for a split second he thought she might wave him off as being silly, but she didn't. The corners of her mouth shifted slightly as she took hold of his hand.

Twirling her into the fold of his arms, he swayed with the rhythm, thankful for the spacious kitchen, ignoring Sister Mary Rose's admonition to always leave enough space when dancing for the Holy Ghost. Eileen fit perfectly against him. If she'd lean in a little closer, her head would tuck in perfectly under his chin.

Right now, more than anything he wanted to pull her more closely against him. Instead he twirled her out and around, and when she returned once again curling into his shoulder, he slowed his steps, breathing in the scent of her, savoring the feel of her.

The final chorus played. The recorded Eileen of years ago sang out loud and strong, hanging on every beat. Sean wished this song, this moment could go on forever. Brother was he in trouble. Especially if he did what he was thinking. Wanting. The music stopped. The room fell into heavy silence. The only thing he could hear was the beat of his own heart, and then, the piercing shrill of the weather alert radio.

Pulling apart, he lowered his eyes and stepped back. Both their voices tumbling over each other, "Tornado."

• • • •

"Tornado Warning." Ethan sprang from his spot on the sofa.

Fancy blinked. "Tornado?"

"Warning," Ethan repeated.

Fancy turned to Garrett who merely waved his hands and shrugged.

"Laundry room. Now." Meg pointed down the hall, spun around and hurried to the base of the stairs in time to see Glenn tearing down the steps.

"Is that what I think it is?" he asked, following Meg back to the kitchen.

Allison looked to the staircase. "Anyone else in the house?"

"No." Without slowing, Meg grabbed a flashlight from above a shelf in the kitchen and kept moving. "Everyone else checked out by lunchtime."

Following the crowd, Fancy figured this was something like earthquakes in California, only instead of standing in a doorway they were heading for the laundry room. That part she wasn't terribly sure of why.

Her confusion must have shown on her face. The second she crossed the doorway into the surprisingly large laundry room, Ethan closed the door behind them and explained, "Tornado watch means that the weather conditions are good for tornadoes. Warning means one's been spotted nearby and we need to take cover."

"The laundry room," she mumbled.

"For us, yes," Meg said. "It's the only windowless room in the center of the house on the first level. Some of the old ranch houses have actual storm cellars, but this is the best we have."

In the closed room, Fancy stood against the wall to one side of her and with Garrett on the other.

Opening cabinet doors that revealed a large storage closet, Meg pulled out multiple cushions, blankets, and more flashlights. "If anyone gets hungry I have snacks and water in here too."

"How long do you expect to be stuck here?" Garrett asked.

Arms laden down with more cushions, Meg spun her head over her shoulder. "If the tornado doesn't reach us, not long. Maybe less than an hour till we get the all clear."

"And if it does reach us?" Fancy found the idea of a tornado even more unsettling than earthquakes.

Ethan, Allison and Meg exchanged a quick glance, but Ethan was the one who answered, "Pray for the best."

"What about Adam?" Fancy's gaze shot to the closed door.

Meg set what looked like outdoor patio cushions on the ground. "He'll be hunkered down at the clinic with his staff and any animals."

"Oh, the dog," Fancy gasped.

"Dog?" Meg froze mid toss of a cushion. "What dog?"

"The beautiful wolfhound."

This time more than one head spun around to stare at her.

"At first I thought it was a wolf, but he was so friendly and well trained I realized he had to be a cattle dog mix."

At the still stricken look on Meg's face, Fancy continued, "You know, the one that guards the vet offices."

Meg's, "You know where Adam's vet clinic is?" collided with Ethan's, "When did you see this dog?"

Reaching for her hand, Garrett barely covered hers before pulling away and nodding for her to tell her story.

"I guess I should start at the beginning."

"That would be good." Ethan crossed his arms.

Fancy took in the cushions dispersed with blankets, snacks and flashlights on the ground. "We might as well make ourselves comfortable." This was going to take a while.

CHAPTER FOURTEEN

The back door to the ranch banged open and Connor flew in, cradling Stacey in his arms with Catherine on his heels with Brittany snuggled against her. "Paul Brady called to let us know a tornado was spotted just east of his place and it's heading this way."

The occasional need to take cover in the storm cellar was a fact of life that came with living in Tornado Alley. This wouldn't be the first time the Farradays had ridden out a storm in the old cellar. The original homestead had come with a root cellar. Somewhere along the way it was converted to a storm cellar and Sean's father was the one to modernize it into a solid structure that would keep his family safe even if Dorothy and the Wicked Witch of the West came whirling past riding a Kansas Tornado.

Sean narrowed his gaze out the kitchen window. "That sky looks ugly. We'd better hurry."

No sooner had Sean led the way out the back door than the wind that had already been strong enough to carry a hen across the county kicked up a notch, nearly knocking him back into the house. Keeping close to his son and daughter-in-law, Sean looped his arm around Eileen and shuffled them the few feet to cellar doors that nearly swung off the hinges when he pulled them open.

At the same moment, Eileen and Sean glanced up at the nasty clouds. She could almost feel the air still as each of them sucked in a breath and failed to exhale, until they softly muttered, "Oh, shit."

One of the first things she'd learned about storms in Texas was that if you see a tornado moving across the horizon, you'll be fine. On the other hand, if it appears to be standing still, run for the hills as the thing is coming straight at you. This skinny funnel in the distance was dancing in place.

"What about the animals?" Catherine pointed over her shoulder as she descended the steps.

Eileen huddled behind Connor, following Catherine downstairs and not till the doors closed and were bolted behind them did Sean answer. "They're safer in the stalls. If that thing doesn't shift course, the barn might lose a roof but the animals will be mostly safe."

Frowning, it was obvious Catherine believed her father-in-law, but didn't understand why.

"All the senses that tell a horse where to go under normal weather conditions disappear in the turmoil of an impending tornado. On top of that, the flying debris from fence posts and missing roofs can be as deadly as the tornado. They'll be fine where they are."

This was only the third time in all these years since Eileen had moved in that the storm warnings were close enough to send them running to the cellar for cover. Eileen didn't like the anxious feeling anymore now than she had the last two times. Back then the tornadoes had touched down, danced around, but hadn't come close enough to the ranch to do any damage. Except back then she hadn't had time to see one. The hairs on her arm stood upright and an icy chill slid down her spine as unsettling as if someone had dropped a frozen cube along her back.

At this moment she didn't give a hoot about the singing, the show, Glenn or her forgotten dreams. All she wanted was for her family to be safe. Each and every one of them. Her gaze shifted to the man seated beside her, his arm protectively draped around her, his gaze staring up at the doors. Concentration and concern clearly painted on his face. And maybe she wouldn't mind another dance with Sean Farraday.

• • • •

"Living in San Diego had taken my life from bad to worse," Fancy started, ignoring her sister's silent shudder.

Immediately, Ethan enfolded Allison's hand in his.

"That scumbag Damien had me convinced he was my ticket to Hollywood fame and fortune. Even after the first scrape with the drug charges and him dragging me to San Diego, I still believed in him. Was afraid not to." She slipped her hand out from under Garrett's and rubbed both palms against her legs. "I might be a little slow sometimes, but I've never been totally stupid. By the second time I almost wound up in jail taking the rap for him, what little smarts Mama infused in me kicked in."

Allison's heartbroken expression lifted momentarily at the mention of their mother.

"The problem I struggled with was that without Damien, I didn't have any money, any place to go, or anyone to turn to."

"So you wound up at the Salty Dog," Ethan volunteered.

Fancy nodded. Now that her life had become something akin to normal, the idea of that being the first place she thought to go to find a way out actually made her cringe at her own stupidity. Well, maybe not totally stupid. She did find Ethan.

"Desperation makes a person do things no sane human being would. Add that I might have had a little too much to drink." Her gaze shifted to Ethan, silently taking in her side of the story.

Always the gentleman. She'd learned that much about him in the few short days they'd been together. No way would he confirm what she'd skirted around, but he knew she'd been a helluva lot more than tipsy, and truth was, she knew it too, but saying so now came...hard.

Folding her hands in her lap, she noticed a sunflower poster on the wall. So like Meg, pleasant and sunny, even if doing laundry. Keeping her eye on the positive image, she pushed forward with her story. "That's when I found myself having to choose between the lesser of two evils."

Ethan's brow shot up high on his forehead.

His near comical reaction was almost enough to make Fancy smile. Almost. Then her mind flashed back to the sheer terror that had swallowed her whole when she realized there would be no solutions, temporary or otherwise, from the sailor determined to get something for all the booze he'd bought her. "The slobbering drunk with a vicious grip, or the stone-faced mountain of a man with the nerve to take Mr. Grip on."

"I suppose," Ethan hefted one shoulder in a half-hearted shrug, "stone-faced is marginally more flattering than the lesser of two evils."

Fancy couldn't bring herself to smile at the concession. The fear clutching her heart at the moment she'd had to choose came rushing back as noxious and menacing as it had been that fateful night. "Anyhow, I clearly made the right choice, and by the time a few days had passed and I'd moved on to Kathy's house, I had a better sense of what I needed to do. Find a real job even if it meant waiting tables again. Find a real agent if I wanted to give Hollywood one more try, and I did. Only no sooner had I found a job and started the agent hunt again then I realized I was pregnant."

Allison and Ethan nodded in near perfect unison. That made Fancy smile. She wondered if they realized how much they did exactly alike, like a matching set of salt and pepper shakers, or souvenir bobbleheads.

"I thought it was a sign. A new corner. A new me. Only," she sucked in a ragged breath, "it wasn't a new me. It was a scared me. I did my best. I really did. I didn't want anyone else to take care of her. Didn't trust them, but you can't work and take care of a baby. And talk about no sleep. Half the time I wasn't sure if I was coming or going or stuck somewhere in the middle. And I was supposed to keep this up for years to come and still raise her to be smart, and caring, and thoughtful of others. Everything her father was."

The muscles at the base of Ethan's jaw began to twitch in alternating rhythm.

"Everything about your family and home seemed so perfect. Too perfect. But I had to find out. It was easy enough to track the family down from the information you'd given me. So I gathered every cent I had, packed Brittany up into a coughing jalopy I bought and headed east."

"They are," Meg said from across the room. "It's none of my business, but this family is the stuff that movies are made from."

Fancy nodded. So she'd figured out very quickly. "Originally I was only going to ask for help."

"You could have come to me," Ethan added.

"That," she blew out a sigh, "was more challenging. I'd lost the paper you gave me with your contact info and the Marines aren't exactly forthcoming with how to reach out to their servicemen, at least not the ones who they train for things I probably don't want to know about."

Heaving in a deep breath, he dipped his chin once. They both knew she was right.

"And me?" Allison asked.

Fancy's heart tripped at the lost and yet hopeful expression on her sister's face. "South America."

Allison nodded.

"Anyhow, I don't know what I thought I'd find, but not until I pulled into this sleepy little town did I realize it was everything I wanted my daughter to know about life. So I got a room at the bargain motel just outside of Butler Springs and every day I'd come back here and watch."

"Every day?" Ethan asked.

Fancy nodded.

"For how long?" Allison squinted in thought at her sister.

"A week."

"A week." Ethan almost lunged forward. "You stalked my family for a week?"

"Not stalked," she shook her head, "observed. Turns out your brother the vet really would step in front of bus before he'd step on an ant, your brother the police chief plays basketball with some of the local teens on his afternoons off—and by the way, any moron could have seen he was in love with Adam's receptionist. The doctor has the bedside manner of an angel, at least that's what the two ladies at the boutique said. Apparently, he's one notch short of the saint your youngest brother is."

"Not sure I want to know what they said about me." Ethan shifted his weight but never let go of his wife.

Laughing now was easier. Fancy smothered a soft chuckle. "You I already knew about. Anyhow, your aunt has the respect of this entire town and your father is like Roy Rogers, never met a man he didn't like, or who didn't like him. And that's when I knew. The best thing I could do for Brittany—at the time—was give her a normal family like this."

"How do you go from worrying about her every hour to leaving her in a box in front of the police station?" Ethan asked.

"The dog," Fancy answered easily. "The one that sat on Adam's front stoop every morning."

A huge grin bloomed on Meg's face. "Oh, that's going to be

fodder for Joanna and her folklore history of Tuckers Bluff and the ranch."

"Excuse me?" Fancy asked.

Meg waved her hands. "Nothing. Never mind."

"You saw a dog camped out at Adam's every morning?" Ethan asked.

Fancy nodded. "I guess he slept on the porch, then he'd do his perimeter walk around just before the staff arrived. Eventually I'd spot him nearby under a tree or a shrub. Just keeping an eye on the place."

Ethan and Allison shared a sideways glance. They were telling each other something, but Fancy didn't have a clue what.

"I'll tell you one thing, he's a pretty smart dog. A couple of days in he noticed I was watching the clinic and began following me around, kept his distance. When he finally came up close, he'd always park himself close to Brittany. Whether I was keeping an eye on your brothers, or the cafe, didn't matter. Lassie stayed by my side."

"Lassie?" Meg asked.

Fancy smiled. "He reminded me of how Lassie always took care of Timmy. It just fit."

"Hmm," Ethan mumbled.

"Once I made up my mind, I went back to Butler Springs and arranged for all the paperwork so my baby girl could have a good life. Like I said, at the time it never occurred to me I would ever be able to get out of the vicious cycle I'd created for my life. Then I waited for your brother to go into the police station. Made sure everyone was busy enough not to see me through the doors and placed Brittany safely in the entry with Lassie at her side."

Allison's gaze narrowed. "But you left her. In a box."

"Technically yes, but not until I'd seen Declan pick her up and take her inside. I'd had to pawn the car seat and a few other things later that morning for the cash I needed to keep going. I knew her family would take care of everything she needed."

"And the allergies. Why didn't you tell us?" Ethan asked.

That made no sense. "What allergies?"

"She was allergic to the formula DJ bought for her."

"I didn't know."

"How could you not know?"

"I'd nursed her until I left her with your family. The woman at the store who helped me get the formula told me the brand I got was best for babies. It was pricey, but she was worth it."

"It was in a plastic bag."

"Yes," she said. "I'd set it down at the motel on the wet counter. The box was ruined but I put the salvaged formula in a bag. I, uh, didn't have money for a new box."

For a few seconds, her chest tightened at the thought of putting her little girl in harm's way. She could feel Ethan's gaze boring into her, studying her, evaluating, and finally she saw acceptance brush across his face. He believed her.

"What do you want now?" he asked.

Three sharp siren blasts signaled the all clear, but no one moved. All eyes were intent on Fancy, waiting for her response.

Meg and Allison's phones sounded with a text notification, but Ethan's actually rang. Glancing at the number, he swiped at the phone. "What's up?" The muffled sound of a voice on the other end had Ethan springing to his feet and nodding. "On my way."

From the wide-eyed look on Meg and Allison's face, their texts had nothing to do with weather alerts. Or maybe it did.

Already on her feet, Fancy inched closer to Ethan. "What's wrong?"

"At least two tornadoes touched down. One of them at the Brady's, another at the ranch."

"Oh my God." Fancy's heart nearly stopped. "Brittany?"

Ethan shook his head. "No one's answering their phones."

CHAPTER FIFTEEN

The sound of a thundering freight train had all the adults in the shelter hovering more closely over the two little girls. Old enough to understand what was going on, Stacey did her best to keep Brittany entertained and smiling. The doors rattled, Sean leaned even closer between the door and his family, and Eileen said a silent prayer.

More than once she'd heard someone describe a tornado like a train, but she hadn't imagined the impact of the sounds and sensations that came barreling overhead would have on the human body. Terror being the first thing to cross her mind. Visions of every twister movie she'd ever seen with cows and tractors and houses sucked up and tossed through the air like a football on a Saturday afternoon pick up game had her moving even closer to her youngest family members.

The doors were the first to settle into place as the roar of the wind ebbed to near silence. The peaceful quiet was broken by Connor's cell.

"Hello?"

"Is everyone okay?" Desperation laced Adam's tone.

"Yes. So far, so good."

"Who's with you?"

"Catherine, Dad, Aunt Eileen and the girls. We came over when Brady called. Our house doesn't have a storm cellar."

She could almost hear Adam nodding on the other end. "Good. The thing passed the town by. We're all fine."

Sean threw the cellar doors open and carefully climbed up, Connor on his heels. The two men whistled.

"What about the Brady's?" Connor scanned the area. "If the twister they spotted is the same one that blew through here…"

Carrying Brittany in her arms, Eileen popped her head out at the top of the stairs. What a mess. The fencing between theirs and Connor's place was uprooted and tossed around the back field like a childhood game of pickup sticks. Depending on the rest of the pasture fences, they might have their hands full the next few days rounding up stray cattle. Following the edge of their land, the few trees that lined the property were blown over or completely gone. In the distance a vehicle was upside down, wheels up. Connor's truck. Eileen's heart stuttered at the sight.

"It must have blown between us," Sean mumbled softly.

"Has everyone checked in?" Connor asked his brother.

"You guys were the last ones. Your phones weren't working."

"I'm the only one with a cell on me and while the tornado was whizzing by I must not have had a signal."

Adam scoffed on the other end of the line. "No sh…kidding."

"I'll spread the word."

Eileen reached the back door of the house first and rushed to answer the ringing phone. No doubt the entire town would be calling each other to make sure everyone was safe. "Hello?"

"Oh, thank heaven you're all right." It took Eileen a moment to recognize the frantic voice as Sally Mae. "I just drove up the road to check for damage. Oh, lord Eileen. The house is almost gone."

Eileen's heart stopped. She could hear Sally Mae's dog barking and the pounding of foot steps.

"I think they're still inside. We need help. Fast. Y'all are the closest. Bring whoever's home. I'll call DJ next."

"Who's still inside?" All of Eileen's family stood frozen beside her, waiting for word.

"The Bradys. The twister must have buzzed right over their house!"

• • • •

Having filled the back of his pickup with water, blankets, shovels, and any other items needed to dig a family out of a damaged home, Sean Farraday pressed on the gas and practically flew out of the drive, spitting gravel behind him.

"Oh, I hope it's not as bad as Sally Mae made it sound." Eileen sat in the passenger side of the truck. Connor had taken his wife and the two girls back to their house in one of the ranch vehicles and would be loading up and joining the group.

Sean sucked in a deep breath. Mother Nature could be vicious. It had been decades since any serious damage had struck Tuckers Bluff. When he'd pulled Eileen into his arms and swayed to the rhythms of a song long forgotten, of all the possibilities for what would have happened next, digging a friend's family out of their home hadn't been on the list anywhere.

The nearest neighbor, they were still almost a twenty minute drive away. Fifteen at the current speed. When they came over the slight rise in the road that allowed for the first views of the original Brady ranch, Sean felt his heart nearly stop. The beautiful three-story wood siding home was barely a single floor high.

"Oh, no." Eileen breathed from the seat beside him. "They don't have a cellar."

There was no need to answer. They both knew the family would be huddled somewhere under all that mess. Now he had a new dilemma – how to go about freeing his neighbors and keeping Eileen away from crawling all over the dangerous mound of a house in search of the Bradys. Once upon a time Eileen was very much a city girl, but now she could do most anything on the ranch he or any of his sons could do. She was a formidable woman. And going to serve him his backside on a platter when he told her to stay the hell off that house.

● ● ● ●

From the moment Fancy hopped into Adam's truck heading toward the ranch, her heart was thickly lodged in her throat. If she'd thought she'd known fear before, she was dead wrong. Not since the day Brittany was born had Fancy felt the elation that came half way to the family homestead, hearing that all the Farradays had survived the tornado unscathed. Only the following news of a family neighbor in trouble robbed her from smiling like a loon.

"How much farther?" Glenn asked.

"Just around the bend." Adam pointed ahead with his chin.

From what Fancy remembered, just about every road from Dallas to New Mexico was straight and boring. This little corner of the county had to have the only bend in the road for the entire state.

Meg gasped, her hand slowly rising to cover her mouth. Fancy had seen lots of tornado damage photos splashed across the news stations through the years, but the sight of this house that appeared to have been crushed under the foot of a very heavy giant was enough to leave anyone stunned.

Meg, Glenn, and Fancy came with Adam in his truck. Garrett, Jamie, Rick and Brooks led the way in his suburban. From the one-sided conversations she'd heard, she suspected they weren't the only ones on their way.

Sure enough, when they'd turned off the main road, trucks were already parked helter skelter across the front of the property. Brooks came to a screeching halt dead center of what was once a front door and bag in hand, ran to the crowd of people gathered. Adam pulled in behind him. Doors clicked open and slammed shut, and folks jogged toward the house. She hadn't any idea what she could do, but she couldn't sit around and wait.

Rick at his side, Garrett came up behind her. "You okay?"

She nodded. About as okay as anyone could be staring at a squashed home, knowing people were trapped inside. From atop what Fancy was pretty sure used to be the front porch, a man she didn't recognized let out a yell. "Over here."

Immediately people took off in his direction, only a few men daring to climb up.

Aunt Eileen came walking past her. "I'm unloading water from the truck. Want to help?"

"Absolutely." Fancy fell into step beside her. Glenn and Rick hurried in the opposite direction toward the house where a human chain had formed, receiving and hauling debris away from the house where folks hoped to find the family tucked safely below.

"This is my niece. Grace." Aunt Eileen waved from one woman to the other.

The niece. The one that brought Aunt Eileen into the family. In many ways the adult version of her Brittany. "Nice to meet you."

"Likewise," Grace answered. Stopping at the open tailgate she stared blankly at the stacked cases of water and other goods brought from the ranch.

"Grace?"

"Oh." She smiled at her aunt. "Sorry, just contemplating the immortality of the crab."

"Yeah." Eileen's smile seemed rather wistful. "Me too."

Grace let out a soft sigh and turned to her aunt. "Where do you want these?"

"I've set up a table out of the high traffic zone." Eileen handed off a case of water. "Your father wouldn't let me near the building."

"Can't imagine why." Grace bit back a chuckle.

Eileen straightened, her gaze leveling with her niece's, and Fancy would swear the woman was suddenly two inches taller. "Don't *you* start with me."

"Never crossed my mind." Arms weighed down, Grace leaned into her aunt, planting a sweet kiss on her forehead. "Love you just the way you are. If you folks can handle the rest of this alone, I'd like to lend a hand to the clean up crew."

"Go." Eileen turned from her niece to Fancy and crawled up to push the water cases closer to the edge.

"Immortality of the crab?" Fancy asked.

The smile on Eileen's face seemed to rise more easily to her eyes. "It's an expression her mama used all the time. Helen was a fountain of my grandmother's sayings. The ones she said most often were 'walking quickly no one will notice', 'anyone can keep a secret as long as two of them are dead', but the most often repeated fondly by her children is when someone is lost in thought, a person will ask what are you thinking and in remembrance of their mom they'll answer—"

"The immortality of the crab," Fancy finished for her. "But didn't her mom pass away when she was just a baby?"

"She did."

Fancy gave the situation some thought. "And you said you were thinking the same."

"Betty Sue is pregnant. Knowing she, Paul, and their little boy are trapped in that house, and that if one thing goes wrong we could lose either one of them, I'd be lying if I said it didn't make me remember when Helen got sick and we had to face losing her." Eileen cast her gaze to the wind-tossed house. "I'm praying with all that's in me for that family."

It hadn't occurred to Fancy that any of the Farradays would be taken back to the day they'd lost their mom. She should have been more sensitive. And looking at this smart, brave woman, Fancy should have realized sooner how much of today's world held in common with the past. Eileen had raised her sister's daughter, and so far so was Allison.

More cars arrived. Fancy recognized some of the faces. Declan and his wife popped out of a police car and hurried to what was left of the house. The two sisters from the town general store came rushing toward Eileen. The tall one spoke first. "We have fixings for sandwiches and some energy bars in case this goes longer than we'd like."

Aunt Eileen nodded. "They have to be so very careful not to make things worse poking around to find them that digging them out could take a good long while. The building is so unstable only folks with fire department or police training are part of the rescue team scaling what's left of the house."

Or military, Fancy thought. Ethan was right in the thick of things. A small smile teased at one side of her mouth. Rick had joined the reverse bucket brigade passing debris along and away from the house, but Garrett had joined the inner circle of the rescue team doing something with ropes. She'd almost forgotten he'd grown up in a construction family. He really was one of the good guys.

"Great," Eileen answered the two women. "I've set up a couple of tables off to the left. You can work there."

Both sisters bobbed their heads and waddled back to their vehicle.

"They really are sisters?"

Eileen nodded. "Yep. No predicting genetics."

"Suppose not." Another similarity between past and present struck her. Fancy stood face to face with a woman who could sing like an angel and gave up her dream of stage and stardom to raise her sister's children. How wrong was it of Fancy to want both? She hefted a case of water from the car. "You have a great family."

Aunt Eileen hopped off the truck, lifted a case of water, and started back toward the tables. "Thank you. I think so."

"And you never married yourself?"

Eileen's gaze shifted to where Glenn stood with Rick and a few others then shook her head. "Raising seven kids has a way of sucking up all your spare time."

"I bet it does." She looked around at the brothers working side by side. At Ethan's father as strong and handsome and involved as his sons. "Grace is the only girl. The baby."

"Don't let her hear you say that. She'll box anyone's ears who calls her the baby. She doesn't even take well to being described as the youngest."

"No. I bet she doesn't." Fancy set the case of water down and noticed Eileen already had a washtub with ice under the table. "Shall I put these in there?"

"Yes, please."

A loud creaking noise shattered the otherwise quiet evening, followed by a voice yelling "Heads up" and several people freezing in place, balancing, the wood shifting underneath. The house remained still once again and another voice hollered, "We've got to hurry before this whole thing gives way."

"Oh, God," Fancy whispered.

"Yes. Prayers help." Eileen looked up at the sudden burst of activity, her gaze steady and focused and unwavering.

Grace came running back beside her aunt, her expression lighter, and rested an arm across her shoulders. "They found Betty Sue. She should be out very soon."

"Any idea of her condition?" Eileen reached up and squeezed the hand draped over her shoulder.

"Good enough to be talking and directing the rescue team toward her." Grace hesitated, her smile slipped. "They're under a lot of debris."

"Don't you worry. They'll be fine."

That lost in thought gleam appeared again in Grace's eyes, and then squeezing her aunt tightly, Grace mumbled against her aunt's temple, "Love you. I'd better rejoin the debris line."

"Go," Eileen encouraged.

With another nod and a strong shot of the respect Fancy had seen flowing from one member of the family to the other, Grace turned on her heel and hurried back to the crew.

Together Fancy and Eileen went back to the truck for more supplies. Hauling another case from the bed, Fancy turned to the family matriarch. "She turned out to be quite a woman, didn't she?"

Pride beaming from clear blue eyes, Eileen nodded. "They all turned out great."

"Yes. Yes, they did." She considered her next question carefully. "What's it like to raise someone else's child?"

Eileen stopped mid-step, her mouth slightly open, her eyes a little wide, and then exhaling softly, she nodded. "The human heart is an interesting thing. It has the capacity to love endlessly. It doesn't matter if I carried these children in my womb because they've always been under my heart. And," Eileen hefted a crate with blankets and began to walk, "when you think you couldn't possibly love any more, the children of your heart start bringing more children into the family and you realize how much more love you have to give."

"Of course." Fancy watched this family. Children raised by aunts. A daughter still thinking of, no loving, a mother she never knew. Respect and love abounding. So many similarities and yet so different. Fate sure liked messing with her.

CHAPTER SIXTEEN

P aul Brady, his pregnant wife and young son were safe and sound and tucked away at his cousin's house. What was left of the old house that had been in the family for generations was going to have to be razed and rebuilt.

"There's so much to clean up." In the passenger seat, Eileen let out a bone-weary yawn. "It's a miracle that twister didn't do more damage."

"That's for sure." Sean Farraday shifted in his seat. "Looks like the Brady's was the only house caught in the path. Some of the other ranchers have felled trees, torn up fencing, and a little wind damage here or there but it could have been so much worse."

Eileen knew not a single member of the Farraday clan hadn't felt deep down the fear and sorrow of losing a loved one so unexpectedly. Beyond elated wasn't strong enough to describe how she felt that the entire Brady family had been found safely huddled in a bathtub under the protective barrier of a small mattress.

"Paul's brother said they lost a bunch of fencing too." Sean held onto the steering wheel with one hand and rubbed the back of his neck with the other. "I don't want to think about how much fun we're going to have rounding up and sorting cattle."

Even though she hadn't done any of the physical labor involved in digging Paul Brady's family out from under his house, Eileen felt the stress and work she'd done feeding and hydrating what seemed like half of Tuckers Bluff in every sore muscle of her body. "With so many folks needing help with clean up, I should saddle up in the morning and help. Especially since Finn is going to be working with Connor on the roof damage to his stables."

"As much as I'd love to spend the day in a warm jetted tub, I'm afraid you're right. We're going to need all hands on deck to get things back to normal."

"Yep." The adrenaline rush of the crazy evening had long ago crashed. Eileen didn't dare let her head tilt back against the seat or her eyes drift closed for fear she might wind up snoring till morning. Instead she focused on the headlights lighting the way. She was so blasted tired she could barely think straight. And now was certainly not the time to kick around all that had happened over the last couple of days. Not seeing Glenn, not singing to his old arrangements, and certainly not dancing with Sean. How could it be after all these years she'd never danced with Sean? Well, she had danced with him a few times at weddings but those times had always been by strict Irish Catholic standard—him and her and enough room between them for the Holy Ghost. Earlier tonight hadn't left a sliver of room for a holy photograph. And wasn't that food for thought?

• • • •

Glenn slid his shirt over his head and tossed it into the corner. He couldn't remember a day this exhausting in a long while. He'd never met Paul Brady and his family before today and yet, working to remove debris and rubble with the other friends and neighbors from Tuckers Bluff, he couldn't possibly have been more concerned and fretful for them if they'd been his own relatives.

Unwilling to bother with his pants, Glenn collapsed onto the bed. One helluva day. He didn't envy the cleanup ahead of the Brady family. Though from what was explained to him, the family tree had strong roots and lots of branches from which to draw on for assistance.

He still couldn't believe how many people had arrived to help. Every time he glanced toward the main road, more people were coming, and Eileen had taken over as foreman, directing the newcomers to where they could be the most help. This amazing woman never ceased to surprise him. Had she always been so capable? Yes, she'd always had a beautiful voice, and a beautiful heart, but he didn't remember this woman. The strong woman who could probably command a Marine platoon if given the chance. And with a smile too.

The thought actually brought a grin to his face. Thinking of this day and of Eileen made him smile. A smile from deep down in what used to be an aching heart. First he'd need a good night's rest, and then he'd work on making some changes in his world. Changes that would keep him smiling for a long time to come.

• • • •

The to-do list in Sean's mind was growing almost exponentially with every mile they drove. The problem at hand, the only thing he seemed to be able to focus on was the woman across from him in the passenger seat. She'd been a trooper as usual, taking over the directing and nurturing of the friends and neighbors who had dropped everything and come to the aid of the Bradys in a time of need. It was what their community had done for generations and it was one of the things Sean loved about his sister-in-law. And *that* was his problem. Ever since Finn had put the word "love" in Sean's mind, everything involving Eileen seemed to revolve around that one word. He loved how she cared for his family, loved how she dealt with adversity, loved how she could mobilize a team in the face of disaster. All admirable qualities that he might love in one of his sons, neighbors, or dogs.

However, when it came to loving the feel of Eileen in his arms, the sway of her hips against his to the rhythms of the music, and the cute way the corners of her mouth tipped north when something made her happy—that was all Eileen and only Eileen. And now, regardless of Finn's words, Sean was going to have to do something about it.

• • • •

The good thing about spending most of the night tossing and turning is that it made crawling out of bed before dawn to start the day easy. There was no sleep for Eileen to wash out of her eyes. Donning a pair of jeans and work boots, she was in the kitchen packing lunches and scrambling up some breakfast burritos for a light energy boost before everyone headed out the door.

It had been a while since Eileen rode with the family for a work day. Usually she made sure everyone was fed and hydrated and took care of things at home. Today they were spread too thin and there was too much to be done. Already Sean had been on the phone with Sam, who'd reported missing cattle in the pasture closest to his house. Another neighbor, Luke Pendry, also called to say that the tornado had torn a path across his property and the fence between one of his back pastures and Farraday land was down, which meant Pendry and Farraday cattle were most likely off together exploring new territory.

"The horses are loaded in the trailer. We're going to have to go it alone. King is favoring one foot still. I don't want to make it worse." Sean filled his thermos with coffee.

"You have been thinking about retiring him." Eileen took a long gulp of her morning brew. "Maybe it should be sooner than later."

"I was thinking the same thing." Sean blew out a sigh. King was such a great cattle dog, Sean had been slow to bring up a replacement. "Has Finn come out yet?"

"He and Joanna already had their coffee and toast and left for Connor's."

"If this doesn't take near the time I expect it to, I'll go over and lend a hand."

"According to Connor, there's quite the line up of neighbors going to help." She couldn't put her finger on it, but something about the slow way Sean went about his morning routine told her he was either more worried about King than he'd let on, or he hadn't had the best of night's sleep either.

"I was thinking," he reached for one of Eileen's biscuits and slathered on some jam, "might be nice to... uh..." he turned to face her, "go out for a grown up dinner."

Grown up? As compared to what? It's not like they'd taken the kids for Happy Meals at McDonald's on a regular basis. Hell, the nearest McDonald's was all the way in Butler Springs. And it had been a helluva long time since her nephews were kids.

"You know, just the two of us." His gaze seemed to struggle to stay level with hers.

Was he asking her on a date? Because if he wasn't, it sounded suspiciously like one. Did it matter? "Sure," she managed to eke out. Since she'd relived yesterday's dance in her head a hundred times trying to fall asleep last night, going to dinner alone with Sean might stop him from robbing her of more sleep. Or not.

"Friday night?" he asked.

"Sure," she muttered with only a fraction more confidence than the first time.

A smile bloomed on his face. "You ready to go?"

Her mouth muttered, 'yes' but she wasn't all too convinced she was ready for anything reality suddenly seemed to serve up.

The ride to the back pasture wasn't nearly as long in the truck as it would have been on horseback. Sipping coffee made the silence fit. Despite having learned to rise before the sun, Eileen still didn't really wake up until after a few cups of coffee and several hours of daylight.

Parking the truck near the first break in the fence, Sean climbed out and unloaded the horses. Saddled up and riding out on the open field, it hadn't taken long to come across the first stray cows. With the fence down, they were going to need to lead the displaced cattle to the nearest pasture with its fencing intact.

Nudging the horse into a trot, Eileen veered left and Sean turned his horse to the right, ready to gather the cows into a loose herd, except two young bulls picked that moment to butt heads and send the few cows instinctively gathered close scattering in opposite directions. "Marvy," Eileen muttered under her breath. If this was any indication of the rest of the day, it was going to prove to be really, really long.

All they needed were for a few of the animals to move in the right direction and the others would follow. No one wanted to be the last cow left behind. But so far despite pressure from Sean and her, the cows this morning seemed much more interested in grazing than walking.

Sean came up closer. Rather than ride up on her, he slowed, cutting around, encouraging the cow to move just a bit. Once she moved, a couple of cows began following in the right direction. Eileen refrained from letting go of the reins and doing a fist pump. Together they moved slowly alongside the first group, keeping them from moving too fast or stopping to snack.

Not far ahead, they came across a mama and her calf. Eileen went back and forth, seeing one eye than the other until the mama turned toward the rest of the herd. It seemed for every cow that got with the program, another one felt more inclined to wander off. These guys were bound and determined to go in every direction. The short drive seemed to last forever and take even longer. As they approached the next pasture, Eileen could see a mass of cows already huddled waiting for them. Thank heaven at least some of their herd got the memo. Or did they?

Inching forward and back, nipping and barking, she could make out two dogs maneuvering around in the distance, keeping the herd in line.

Eileen trotted closer to Sean and shouted, "Did Luke say anything about bringing his dogs out?"

"Not to me." He shook his head and kept the cows they'd finally corralled moving at a steady pace, his gaze never leaving the small herd of cows ahead ruled by two dogs.

Slow and steady wins the race. They'd read that story to the children growing up and repeated the line a hundred times working the cattle. Yet, right now Eileen was anxious to press her heels into the old mare and gallop ahead to see what the heck was going on.

No sooner had the thought crossed her mind than one of the dogs remained hovering around the small herd in the distance and the other came running in their direction. A few feet closer and she would have had a close up view of the large animal. Instead, it stopped at the head of the gathering of cows and began working them. Still close enough to read Sean's expression, she could see he was clearly as taken aback as she was. The way his one brow went up and he moved close enough for the dog to hear him, she wasn't at all surprised when he began giving commands to the dog, though she hadn't expected the animal to do exactly as told.

"I'll be," Eileen mumbled to herself. Whoever's dogs had come to help, the pups worked those cattle as though they'd been training their entire lives with Sean. He'd always said one good dog could do the work of several good men. It was why he hated to retire King. And this guy was proving to be one very good dog.

Steadily moving the large animals toward the other strays, the dog was impressive, but it was Sean breaking away and riding toward her that she hadn't expected at this point.

Slowly easing her horse in his direction, she came to a stop moments before Sean circled around and stopped at her side, both horses facing the moving cattle.

"Are you seeing this?" he asked.

Did she look blind? "Do you think they belong to Luke?"

Sean shook his head. His face void of any emotion, he turned to her. "Eileen, take a good long look at the dog."

She was the closest she'd been to the cattle dog since his appearance. A bit larger, okay, a lot larger than the border collies they usually used, this pup's colors were becoming clearer. His stance. His face. "Oh, my…"

Sean nodded. This time a hint of a smile teasing his lips. "Looks like Mr. and Mrs. Gray decided to chip in and help."

CHAPTER SEVENTEEN

Butterflies had spent the better part of the morning swooping and fluttering in Fancy's stomach. Allison had agreed to meet with her for coffee. Ethan, along with just about every able-bodied man or woman in town, was off helping clean up from yesterday's storm. Her sister had spent the entire morning treating thankfully minor injuries and was clearly relieved at Fancy's suggestion she pick up something from the café and meet Allison in her office.

Fancy may have made a lot of really stupid decisions as a teen that snowballed into worse choices as a young adult, but she'd always loved and been proud of her baby sister. Now was no exception. "You look exhausted."

"You should have seen me during my residency. *That* was exhausted." Allison stretched left then right and took a seat behind the desk. "Yesterday could have been so much worse."

"It's rather amazing that the Brady's was the only house to take a hit."

"It's even more amazing that trapped under two stories of rubble, the entire family came out dusty but without a single scratch. Not even a broken nail."

Fancy chuckled. "I'm guessing the same can't be said for the folks who dug them out."

"I do believe we had one splinter removal in that group." Allison smiled at her sister. "I still can't believe after all these years I finally get to see you."

"I'm sorry." Fancy had truly thought it for the best at first, then she'd been in so much trouble back to back that she didn't want to taint Allison with the same brush. "I really am."

"I'm delighted to see you looking so good. Guess I can stop worrying."

"You can." Enough time had passed that Fancy was sure this life was going to work. For the first time ever, she even had a savings account and was hunting for her own home.

"So," Allison tossed a pen on the desk and leaned back in her chair, "what happens now?"

"I've already told you I'd like to be a part of Brittany's life now that things are more settled and I have a solid financial footing."

Fancy could see Allison swallow hard.

"I know I signed away my parental rights."

Allison released the slightest of relieved breaths.

"But I'd hoped… well, I had hoped you would reconsider."

"Fancy," Allison folded her hands and leaned forward on her desk, "how much do you love that child?"

"More than my own life."

"And how much do you care about her future?"

Fancy smiled. If med school hadn't worked out, maybe her sister could have been a lawyer. "Enough to let her go."

"But you just said…" Allison stuttered.

"I did." Fancy cut her off. "But that was before."

"Before?"

"I suppose deep down I had my doubts. For months now things have gone so well. Everything with the band is perfect. They're like family to me. Garrett has been such a good friend, so supportive. Now seemed like the right time to make a change. Before Brittany was old enough to truly understand what has been happening."

"What exactly do you think is happening, Fancy?"

"Not what I thought. That's for sure." Fancy dug deep for strength. She'd done this before and it was time to do it again. "I got to spend a few minutes with Grace helping her aunt. It struck me, the similarities in our lives. More importantly, it surprised me how much it shows that she cares for a mother she never knew."

Allison nodded. No doubt everyone in town knew more about the Farradays than Fancy could possibly learn during short visits. "Some days, I still miss Mom, but Aunt Eileen has a way of filling big shoes."

"I noticed. And honestly, I miss Mom all the time. Have for decades. It's one of the reasons I came back. When I signed Brittany over, I never thought I'd have anything close to a normal life."

"I'm guessing there are a lot of people who would not consider performing all over the country normal."

"At least I'm not living out of cars and following all the wrong men around the country."

Allison lifted a single brow.

"I don't mean Ethan. I meant the loser who stole my car and left me stranded in Alabama."

This time both of Allison's brows flew high on her forehead.

"I'd made a terrible mistake taking off with him. We'd barely crossed the state line when I'd changed my mind about him. Still regret even a minute wasted with that creep."

"Hang on." Eyes drawn close together, Allison's brows were getting a workout today. "When did you change your mind about leaving Brittany with Ethan?"

"It was always a hard choice, but it wasn't until recently that I believed I could give her a good life too."

"So, those texts you sent me and Ethan. From Alabama. They were about—"

"The creep." Fancy nodded. "I was starting to feel a bit desperate. Desperate enough to ask you to come get me."

"Why didn't you?"

"Garrett. I'd been singing karaoke the night the creep took off. They'd just lost a backup singer and they offered me the job."

Allison sat back in her seat. "Looks like you have a knack for finding knights in shining armor."

"At least twice, yeah. I guess."

"How close are you and Garrett?"

Fancy waved her sister off. "It's not like that. He's just a good friend. My best friend actually."

"You sure?"

"Absolutely. But he's definitely a good influence. If not for him I don't know that I would have ever come to think—hope—that maybe now I could be more of a mother to Brittany." Fancy startled at Allison's sharp intake of breath and shaking her hands quickly explained. "But I realized today she can have two mothers, even if one is her aunt."

Relief washed over Allison's face. "I've seen how the kids love

Eileen. Hell, I haven't been a part of this family for very long and yet that woman has shown me more love and affection than Aunt Millicent ever did. Having Brittany grow up to love me like that would be a good thing."

"About that. I was thinking, it means a lot to me to be a part of my daughter's life. Visit when I can. Have her visit me when she's a little older. Do the internet chatting like military parents do when they're deployed."

Allison nodded. Silently waiting for the next shoe to fall.

"But..." This was hard for her to formulate the words. "I think it would be good for her to think of you as her mother. I can be the crazy talented aunt who swoops in from time to time with elaborate over-the-top gifts and spoil her rotten."

"You want me to pretend to be her mother?"

"Not pretend exactly. Just be. After all, you already are for all intents and purposes."

Allison shook her head. "I can't do that."

"Which part?"

"You're her mama. Aunt Eileen may have been a mother to Grace all of her life, but Grace knew who her mother was. No matter what she calls me now, so will Brittany."

"But—"

"So. Will. Brittany." Allison sighed. "There's a photo of you I got from the internet. It's in Brittany's room. We've taken to calling you Mama Fancy."

"Mama Fancy," she repeated under her breath. She liked the sound of it.

"When Brittany's old enough, we'll find the words to explain." Allison leaned back, her head briefly leaning against her seat. "But you're her mother and nothing is going to change that."

No, she blinked back tears, nothing she did, good or bad, or would ever change that.

● ● ● ●

The long hot shower wasn't enough to undo the tightness in Eileen's back. Sure, she'd been on a horse from time to time, but it had been eons since she'd made an hours long effort to help move cattle. Her designated job at the ranch—if she worked the cattle—was gate keeper. She couldn't get into much trouble with that assignment. Though today she was rather proud of herself. She'd come a long way from the woman who couldn't even climb onto a horse, never mind work on it.

"Thanks." Showered and changed, Sean came down off the bottom step. "I can't believe how quickly we rounded up the missing cattle."

"We were even able to separate our stock from Luke's without his help. Those dogs were amazing. They must belong to someone." Eileen stretched her shoulders and opened the back freezer door.

Sean walked up behind her, his hand gently touching her arm. "First, I can't believe anyone with dogs that smart, that valuable would just allow them to wander around the county all this time. And second, it's been a long, hard day for you. Why don't we go have dinner at the pub? I think a good corned beef and dark ale are in order."

There wasn't much to throwing a casserole in the oven to warm, but the idea of not doing another blessed thing the rest of the night did her aching back good. "Sounds great."

Apparently they weren't the only ones with the idea of heading to the pub. Finn and Joanna drove the ranch truck and she and Sean drove Glenn's car. By the time they crossed the threshold Eileen could already see most of the tables were occupied. "Oh, I hope this keeps up after opening week."

"Ditto," Sean added. "Anyone know how the café is doing?"

"Business as usual." DJ walked in behind them, his eyes scanning from one end of the pub to the other.

"Good." Sean nodded. "None of us want to hurt Abbie's business. You getting off duty?"

"Just making rounds, checking on everyone." DJ's gaze narrowed. "Awful lot of new faces."

The door behind them opened again and this time Fancy and her crew, with Glenn in tow, squirmed their way in. "Standing room only is always a good thing," one of the group said on a laugh.

"We've got plenty of space," Beverly, the wife of the new craft brewer, smiled at the group. "How many will that be?"

Eileen counted over her shoulder quickly. "Looks like eight of us. For now, at least."

"Follow me." Beverly smiled and waved them forward.

"I didn't know you'd be working here," Eileen said.

"Only this week. Though it if this keeps up, Jamie may have to consider hiring a full-time hostess."

Eileen stopped at the table and Glenn and Sean both grabbed for the back of her chair. "Thank you." She smiled to her left then right.

"This seriously reminds me of being in Ireland." Rick took in his surroundings as if it had been the first time.

Eileen leaned forward. "You've been to Ireland a lot, have you?"

"Nope. Only seen it in movies." He eased back in his seat. "And this place looks like every movie I've ever seen with a pub."

The comment got a chuckle from a few folks at the table, but Glenn merely rolled his eyes. "I'll give you it certainly looks like the only Irish pub I've ever been in. That is, the only Irish pub in Ireland."

"When would that have been?" Eileen asked.

For a moment Glenn seemed to almost regret his words before regaining his casual expression. "The group played in Dublin one night during a European tour. Before the girls were born."

That would have been with Sally as lead singer after the group had become rather well known. Around that time Eileen was probably baking cupcakes for kindergarten class or helping with someone's fifth grade science project.

"Well, that would explain your kinship with that piano." Garrett tipped his head toward the stage across the way. "Who'd you play with?"

Glenn smiled and shook his head. "No one you'd know. Just a little jazz band."

It was Rick who looked from Glenn to Eileen and back. Blinked. Dropped his mouth open then snapped it shut. "Holy Sassafras."

"What?" Garrett leaned forward, his expression dripping with concern. "What is it?"

"You're Glenn Baker." Not waiting for a reply, Rick turned to her. "And you're Eileen Callahan. I should have realized it the minute you started singing, but I admit it's been a while since I've heard your album."

"You've heard our album?" Surprise showed easily on Glenn's face.

"My dad wore the thing out. I was weaned on all the jazz greats. Mom was more the country fan. Probably why I love music so much myself." Rick turned to face Eileen. "Please forgive me for not recognizing those golden pipes."

When she sang with the group, the band hadn't been well known enough for folks to recognize her. This was a first. "Golden pipes?"

"Those vocals. I can't believe I didn't recognize you."

Eileen almost laughed. "Not as much as I can't believe you *did*." All in all, this was proving to be a rather surreal week. Deep inside she wondered if when she woke up in the morning she was going to discover all of this had been an odd, inexplicable, crazy dream.

As the waitress walked around the table taking orders, Eileen watched the young band set up. She hadn't realized that Jamie had hired entertainment for the entire week as well. They did a sound check and she ordered the corned beef, immediately returning her attention to the group. A simple five-piece band. Piano, base, drums, saxophone and singer. If she considered the fiddle beside the singer as well, maybe it was a five-person, six-piece band. Though she didn't know that many bands that had fiddle and saxophone players.

"Ladies and gentlemen, welcome to O'Fearadaigh's." A pretty brunette who looked to be about Grace's age stood microphone to her mouth. "For our first number we'd like to do a fan favorite."

It took Eileen all of three notes to recognize "The Devil Went Down to Georgia." By the end of the first verse the entire restaurant was tapping their toes and singing along. The woman had a great way with the fiddle and bow.

"She's good." Garrett leaned into Fancy. "Very good."

"Do you have a fiddler in the group?" Eileen asked.

Garrett nodded. "We do, but Jim is growing tired of touring."

"I don't know that I'll ever grow tired of it." Fancy kept her gaze on the band members, singing along softly under her breath.

When the song came to an end they slid immediately into another tune that Eileen recognized as a recent hit of Fancy's group.

"Okay, she may be better than good." Garrett leaned into hearing distance of Eileen and Fancy, reaching for Fancy's hand, but quickly pulling back before anyone else had noticed the aborted effort. The simple gesture caught Eileen's eye. She'd noticed similar efforts from time to time. The two shared a comfortable familiarity. One she very much understood.

By the time dinner was served the group had taken a break and Garrett and Rick walked over to talk to them. Eileen wouldn't have minded being a fly on the wall in that corner of the pub. She watched heads bob, jaws drop, smiles broaden and finally hugs and handshakes before the two men made their way back to the table.

The next time the musicians took the stage the young singer / fiddle player was beaming like a New England lighthouse. "Folks, we have a special treat for you tonight. In our audience we have a few of the members of Tow the Line."

Several hoots and hollers escaped from around the room.

"And perhaps with a little audience encouragement we can persuade them to join us for a song." She clapped her hands together and within minutes the thunder of applause and whistles could probably have been heard all the way in Dallas.

Fancy shook her head, but Garrett patted her shoulder and nodded. Maybe they'd come to some agreement before. Perhaps this was a live audition of sorts for the young band. How well could they blend without practice. Or maybe it was just a star struck kid's enthusiasm at having a chart-topping band in the audience.

Fancy took hold of the microphone, kicked the cord behind her and Eileen swore that woman lit up from within. "Ladies and Gentlemen, this is what we call a Texas foot stomping and hand clapping kind of song. So put your hands together for me." She clapped her hands in front of her until the audience kept rhythm with her. Then Rick at the piano started to fiddle with the keys. When the base guitarist played a few notes, the entire room recognized the tune and the foot stomping began in earnest as Garrett and Fancy sang the namesake first line of "If You're Going to Play in Texas."

The group played two more songs together with Fancy and the others before flushed, breathing hard, and glowing brightly, Fancy took her seat, not caring her supper had grown cold.

"I can see you love what you do." To Eileen, until now Fancy had looked mostly content, but now, on stage, Eileen recognized the look in Fancy's eyes. She relished every second of it.

"I do." Fancy cut into her meat and smiled. "There's nothing else like it in the world."

Eileen nodded. The electricity in the air was palpable. She could feel the adrenaline rush from merely having Fancy seated beside her. No, she thought, there's nothing like it in the world.

CHAPTER EIGHTEEN

How could he compete with this? Sean had watched the look on Eileen's face with every note Fancy sang. From one song to the next he could feel the energy rise in the room, see the pleasure on Fancy's face and debated did he have the right to try and deprive Eileen of that pleasure, that joy, her dream.

Rick stood from the piano and reached for the mic. "Folks, there's one more surprise for y'all tonight."

Forks clanked on plates and smiling faces turned to the man on stage.

"I grew up in a house filled with music. Two of the stars from one of my father's and my favorite jazz groups are here tonight. Please put your hands together one more time and help me welcome Glenn Baker and Eileen Callahan to the stage."

The unified gasp from the locals in the audience could have been heard across the street. Butler County in on the recent news of Eileen's singing past or the return of her one-time fiancé.

Glenn stretched his hand out for Eileen and when she slid it into his and smiled, Sean asked himself one more time, how could he compete?

Rick shifted to the drums as Glenn squeezed Eileen's hand then slipped away to take his seat at the piano. Eileen's smile grew shaky and she sucked in a slow, deep breath before closing her eyes to the sounds of Glenn playing. The drums and the piano worked together with Eileen's snapping fingers. They were going to do her signature song, "Somewhere." The hairs on his arm stood on end. This would be the first time Sean would hear her sing it live. His heart rate picked up speed. Lord she looked beautiful under those lights. He swallowed a soft laugh. Who was he kidding? She looked beautiful under any light.

She sang the first line and the five simple words "there's a place for us" squeezed his heart. Would there be? Could there be? Had his own blindness to see what was in front of his nose all these years cost him a second chance at true love and happiness?

"You okay, Dad?" Not Finn this time but Joanna leaned over and touched his arm. "You look a little peaked."

"I'm fine."

His latest daughter-in-law studied him carefully before nodding acceptance of his statement and leaning back slightly. "Aunt Eileen really is amazing."

That word seemed to be popping up rather often the last few days. She'd been amazing for a lot longer than that. Stepping in to take care of his children when Helen left them so unexpectedly. Working with him side by side on anything from crossword puzzles and Sudoku to wrangling cattle or waiting up all night for a child to return from a first date, or one who was sick with the flu or chicken pox. Through thick and thin. Good, bad, happy, sad. She'd always been amazing. And wasn't he the biggest idiot for not saying so a hell of a lot sooner.

• • • •

Glenn was in the groove. Once he'd made the decision to give up the business to spend what time Sally had left with her, he'd hardly ever sat down at a piano. After she passed, that world had seemed so far behind. He'd actually forgotten the feel of real keys beneath his fingers. The tingling thrill of each note shattering the silence. And this.

The arrangements that were all theirs. The voice that was irreplaceable. Yes, Sally was the strongest of the backups, and yes, the group did well with her, but her voice didn't stand out the way Eileen's had. What had the other kid said… *golden pipes*. Now Glenn had gooseflesh listening to her belt out the tune that so many remembered. The song that Sally refused to sing no matter how many pleas from the audience. Eileen's song.

Breathtaking wasn't strong enough to describe the range in Eileen's voice. Having hit the high notes in the middle of the song, she pulled the mic from the stand, walking across the stage allowing for Rick and Glenn to have their instrument solos. On cue with no evidence that this routine hadn't been practiced or played in over twenty-five years, she practically made love to the mic, her voice dropped low in her chest, the words coming out a near whisper, slowly building the chorus again, louder, stronger. "Somehow." The note carrying out so powerfully he could almost hear the audience's intake of breath. "Someday." Again, the notes Sally never could hit. Not a murmur in the audience. Eileen had every last person's full attention. Eyes closed, cradling the hand-held mic, her free arm open to the crowds in front of her, smoothly, easily, she delivered the last lyric. "Somewhere."

On the final note the entire house sprang to their feet. Glenn hadn't heard applause like that, well since the last time they'd performed the song. Pushing to his feet, he bent slightly at the waist, gave a short wave to Rick who had handled the drums admirably. The kid knew exactly what the arrangement had called for. Then Glenn moved his arm to Eileen and the place erupted in a second wave of ovation. This, this was why their group was wanted on the television special. This iconic performance was seared in the hearts of generations of jazz fans.

Smiling, Eileen scanned the crowd from left to right. For a few seconds she almost seemed to have forgotten where she was. Her gaze landed on the table off to one side where her family and friends sat. Lingering, her smile lifted and a genuine sparkle reached her eyes. She took another bow and, sliding the mic back into place, hurried off stage, not back to the table as he would have expected but to the side and around the corner. Out of sight of the still applauding audience.

For a moment Glenn wondered if there was something around the corner she needed, or merely the habit of years of performances where they'd exited to whatever dressing room arrangements they'd been given. Whichever, he wasn't leaving her alone. Not again.

Following her wake around the corner to the back he spotted the arrow overhead to the restrooms. At the end of the darkened hall, there she was. Against the wall. Palms flat behind her. Eyes closed. Head tipped back barely resting against the old knotty pine paneling. A single canned light shone above her. She looked like an angel. A singer in the last scene of a soon to be famous movie. More than twenty-five years may have passed but all he saw was the young woman he'd fallen so head over heels in love with.

"You were great," he practically whispered, moving forward.

Turning to face him, she lifted one corner of her mouth in a weak smile. "Thanks."

"They loved you."

"Us."

"No. Had I played a solo of that song the reaction would have been nice and pleasant but it's definitely you they loved."

Her smile grew a little stronger. "It was something."

"You were in your element. No one would guess you haven't been on a professional stage in decades."

"Thanks for the reminder," she chuckled softly.

Coming to a stop in front of her, he reached down and took hold of her hand, cradling it in both of his. "I suspect every man in that room is now just a little in love with you."

Her head finally lifted away from the wall, her gaze leveling with his. "Is that what happened with us? Was it this?" She waved her free hand toward the opposite end of the hall and the still murmuring patrons. "Was this all we truly had?"

The question caught him off guard. He had never considered the possibility that he'd been anything but madly and deeply in love with her. Even when he'd fallen for Sally, built a life with her. A good one. He'd never thought it made what he'd had with Eileen anything less than two people in the right place at the wrong time.

Now here they were. The same two people. A different place and very different time. But the energy, the blood pounding through his veins, and the beautiful woman with the golden voice and penetrating blue eyes was very real. Closing in another half step, ignoring the flash of surprise in her gaze, he had to do what had been in the back of his mind since he saw her at the table that very first night and had been slowly pushing its way to the forefront of his thoughts. Lowering his head, almost directed by the familiarity of a long ago memory, his lips touched hers. Coming home.

• • • •

On stage, singing, the lights low, the music so familiar, the energy, the adrenaline, Eileen shuddered. For days she'd been inundated with forgotten memories and sensations. Tonight, out there, it had all come flooding back. Every second of all those years. She wasn't even here in Tuckers Bluff, she was in New York, or Philly, or Tucson, or Miami. So many years had slipped away. Then, on a natural high from the applause, her gaze fell on Sean, Finn, and Ethan who had joined the table.

The next twenty-five years paraded through her mind in the following instant. She needed a minute. Air. Maybe a drink.

In the fog of the dim light, Glenn appeared. Tall, handsome, talented, still sexy. A few words passed. Like a Sunday comic strip, a light bulb of understanding illuminated the memories and feelings ricocheting about in her head. And then the ghost of her past leaned forward and touched his lips to hers. Slow, steady, soft and caring.

He was kissing her. She should move. Lift her arms. Tilt her head. Something. It had been so very long since she'd been kissed by a man who wasn't blood related and aiming for her cheek. But instinct didn't take over. Her head continued to bat around the thoughts and feelings rushing to the surface. Foremost in her mind—she'd rather be dancing with Sean.

Sean? That had her head springing back like a snapped rubber band.

His one arm over her shoulder, palm against the wall for balance, Glenn stared at her through narrowed eyes. Booted heels clicked against the old wood floors and Glenn jolted back to the opposite wall.

Eyes level, Eileen did her best to read the thoughts scrambling behind the stormy gaze. She could read Sean and the boys with the same ease she'd unravel words on a printed page, but this man, she had no idea if his thoughts were good, bad, or neither of the above.

Sean came to a stop midway between her and Glenn. His gaze scanned the situation. Teeth clamped shut, a muscle in his jaw twitched before his throat cleared. "Thought I'd come see if everything was all right."

A lot of answers shouted at Eileen, but *all right* was most definitely not one of them.

• • • •

"Wow." Fancy turned to Garrett. "Just wow."

"I thought she'd knocked it out of the park the last time we heard her. This is like over the green monster, out of the park, across town, and on a highway to heaven."

Joanna chuckled. "You may have missed your calling as a writer."

"Do songs count?" Garrett asked.

"Absolutely," Joanna confirmed.

"So," Fancy looked to the hall where Eileen had disappeared and Ethan's father had followed, "haven't known the family very long, but should someone maybe go see what's going on back there?"

Finn shook his head. "Nope. They're all grown up. It's time they figured this out for themselves."

"This?" Ethan asked. "I know I've been a little preoccupied, but what exactly is this?"

Finn shrugged.

"Sometimes being a grown up isn't enough." Fancy reached out for her sister's hand. She'd arrived in Tuckers Bluff filled with high hopes, doubts and more fear than she knew how to deal with. She should have realized her baby sister would be smart enough to sort it all out and make Fancy see things were exactly as they were meant to be. Mama Fancy suited her just fine. "Every once in a while we need our family to kick our butts."

"Well, I couldn't have kicked him any harder if I'd worn steel tipped boots."

"What did you do?" Ethan frowned at him.

Finn shrugged. "Nothing much. Just told Dad if he didn't like Glenn making a move on Aunt Eileen then maybe he should."

"What?" Ethan nearly spit out his beer.

"Oh, put your eyes back in your head. Y'all have seen them in action for as long as I have. Until now it wasn't our place to say anything."

"Not sure it is now either," Ethan mumbled.

A nearby chair scraped across the floor and Fancy turned to see DJ spinning it around and taking a seat at the table then toss a piece of paper onto the table. "Report's in."

"And?" the two brothers echoed.

"The guy is so squeaky clean I could wash my windows with him."

Allison and Joanna leaned back in their seats and both women crossed their arms and sported told-you-so grins.

"Don't look at me like that." DJ hung his wrists over the back of the chair. "We couldn't take a risk."

Blowing out a heavy breath, Allison unfolded her arms and leaned forward. "Sometimes I think y'all watch too many shoot 'em up conspiracy movies, but what's done is done. Now what are you going to do?"

DJ shrugged. Ethan fiddled with the label corner on his beer bottle. It was the younger brother who smiled and tipped his longneck at his brothers. "Told ya. It's up to Dad now."

CHAPTER NINETEEN

The air in the narrow back hallway felt thicker than swamp air after a storm. The gentleman in Sean told him to let the lady and her fellow finish their business. The man in Sean wanted to see how many of Glenn's teeth he could knock out with a single right cross.

"I think," Glenn eased slightly to one side, closer to Sean, "I should get back to the table." His gaze lifted to Sean then back to Eileen. "You're in good hands." Turning in place, he nodded curtly to Sean and walked away.

Stepping closer, daring to gently let his fingers rest on her arm, he repeated, "Are you all right?"

"I don't know." She shifted away from the wall to face him, one hand landing flat against his chest. "I honestly don't know."

Heat from her fingertips seeped through his shirt, his chest, and seared his heart. "Eileen—"

She lifted her finger to his lips and shook her head. "Would you do one thing for me?"

He nodded.

"And promise not to hold it against me?"

A spark of fear poked at him from inside, but whatever she wanted from him, whether it was freedom to travel around the world entertaining the masses, or his blessing to return to the man she almost married, for her he'd do anything. Her finger still on his lips, he bobbed his head.

Her finger slipped away. "Kiss me like you mean it."

His head tipped forward, his eyes leveled with hers and if he was dreaming all of this, he hoped to high heaven that he never had to wake up. Taking his time, ignoring the need to brand her as his, he slid an arm around her waist, pulled her close enough that she could probably feel his heart pounding against his rib cage, and let his lips touch hers.

The world spun into its own orbit. Outside noises dimmed to the hum of two hearts beating in time. Toes curled. Heat flared. And he never wanted to stop. Everything about this moment felt perfectly right.

A throat cleared in the distance. Eileen's fingers twirled a lazy circle at the base of his neck and he pulled her even closer.

Louder and more forced, another throat cleared, followed by a feminine gasp. Alarms in the back of his head flashed warning beacons.

A burst of laughter overrode all other sounds, followed by Finn's familiar voice muttering, "Told ya Dad could handle it."

"But…" Ethan muttered, followed by DJ's "I'll be damned," and Connor's "About time."

They were in a public place. A family place. And none of what Sean wanted to do next was intended for public display.

"Okay, boys, give them some privacy," Allison's voice drifted down the hall.

"Like the man said," Joanna joined her sister-in-law, "Dad can handle this. He doesn't need a cheerleading squad."

Bless his daughters-in-law.

Letting his forehead rest on hers, unable to release his hold on her, he swallowed a deep breath. "Was that what you wanted?"

"Mm," she mumbled, slowly opening her eyes to look at him. "Could we, uh, do it again?"

His heart did a somersault. "I'd like to say yes, but I think we need to give Jamison back his hallway."

Eileen turned her head toward the other end of the hall and muffled a smile at the sight of Allison and Joanna's backs ushering his muttering sons over to the table. "They're going to be impossible about this."

"They are." He couldn't stop himself from smiling. "Are we really going to do this?"

Her head bobbed. "I'd sure like to try."

For a moment he wasn't sure what exactly it was she wanted to try, them or singing or both. Not that it mattered. If she wanted to sing in Timbuktu, he'd be right there cheering her on. "Are you going to sing again?"

Still in the fold of his heat, she nodded.

He'd been expecting that. He could work with it. As long as there was a chance for them.

"I want to do the reunion show."

He waited for the other shoe.

"But that's all I want."

Not fully understanding, he leaned back a bit to see her eyes.

"I'm not that person anymore. I love this life. The ranch, the kids, their wives, the next generation, even the stubborn cows." She chuckled a second then straightened her spine and sucked in another breath that made her chest rise and fall and him nearly swallow his tongue. "And, I think, you."

• • • •

Oh lord how she wished her heart would stop battering her ribs like an angry ram. She'd done it. She'd gone after what she really wanted, put her heart on the line, and now she wasn't sure she could take another breath without her heart hurting.

"Eileen." Sean blinked, looked to his left and down the hall, then back. "I don't think anything."

Her breath caught in her throat.

"I know I love you." He swallowed hard. "However long you need. Whatever time you want. I'm willing to work at this until you too know for sure."

Eileen almost laughed out loud. "Don't you think over twenty-five years has been long enough?"

His brows dipped in a confused V, Sean tilted his head. "What are you saying?"

"I think this is a whole lot of change in a very short time."

This time his cheeks pulled with amusement. "You mean more than twenty-five years short?"

"I mean this week. My eyes have been opened. I'd like to give us a little—and I mean little—bit of time to make sure we haven't both lost our minds."

"I can agree to that." He smiled at her. The full wattage smile all his sons had inherited from him. "How little?"

"Not very much." She grinned up at him. "I'd say let's hold off on telling the rest of the family, but I suspect by now every last one of them knows."

A burst of laughter erupted from deep in Sean's chest. "Honey, I think they all knew about it long before we did."

Honey. The endearment played around in her head. She liked it. Yep. Life was about to get a whole lot sweeter.

● ● ● ●

Despite locking lips in the hallway like they'd been the only two people in the pub, Eileen and Sean returned to the table side by side but slightly apart, the same way they might have any other day of the week. And same as he would have any other day of the week, Sean held her chair for her and went to the bar to order her a fresh drink. In so many ways knowing each other so well would make things so much easier, and possibly so much harder. She wanted to try very hard to get this right. Without the entire town gossiping about them.

The band struck up a familiar tune and everyone, except for Sean still at the bar and Rick at the other end of the table chatting away with a couple of ladies at the next table, had gone off to dance leaving her and Glenn alone in a packed room.

"I, uh," he started over her, "uhm about."

"You first," they echoed, then smiled.

"I apologize for kissing you before." Glenn glanced at the dance floor and back. "I admit that the last few days it was fun being together. Re-covering common ground. All the energy and fire in performing again." He sighed. "I guess I got a little carried away confusing feeling alive again with—"

"Feeling love?" she asked.

He nodded.

"Sort of like kissing your sister?" She bit back a smile. As shocked as she'd been, she was alert enough to recognize the difference in his reaction to her kiss versus Sean's. Glenn hadn't had one.

Heat rising in his cheeks, he nodded again. "Hadn't seen that coming."

"Friends then?" She shot her hand out to him.

"Friends." Glenn accepted the hand and gave a single firm shake. "Will you do the show?"

For a single performance, doing this one last time would be fun. "Absolutely. Will you be sticking around a little longer?"

"Nah." He smiled at her. "I'd like to get home. See my daughters. Start on the final details for the show and there's an old coot at my summer lake house who I owe a few hands of cards."

"Sounds good."

"Yes. Yes, it does. Thank you."

Her gaze shifted to Sean walking toward the table, two drinks in hand, then back to Glenn. "No." She patted his hand. "Thank you."

Sean took a seat and Glenn pushed away from the table. "If you two will excuse me, I have a show that still needs some details worked out. Thanks for dropping off the car."

"No problem," Eileen answered.

"None at all," Sean concurred.

"Very well, then." Glenn waved goodbye, slapped Rick on the shoulder on the way out, and just as quickly as he'd waltzed back into her life, he'd waltzed back out.

"That was fun." Fancy took a long sip of her ice water before collapsing into her seat. "I'm usually the one on stage, not the one dancing."

"Tell me about it," Eileen laughed.

"If y'all will excuse me for a minute, I'm going to use the ladies room."

Garrett stood, watched Fancy disappear through the array of tables, then retook his seat beside Eileen.

Leaning away from Sean, who was now talking with Rick about the pros and cons of summer and fall calving, though she had no idea why Rick the musician would care, she faced Garrett. "I'm at that age where I can get away with saying anything I want."

Garrett smiled. "You strike me as someone who got away with whatever you wanted from the cradle. Which, by the way, you're barely out of."

"Oh," she grinned, "a charmer."

He shook his head and tinkered with a cocktail napkin. "Not

really."

"Does she know?"

His gaze shot from the distraction on the table to hers.

"That you're in love with her?" As if he didn't know what she was talking about.

He shook his head. "No. It's not like that—" His gaze returned to the table and he sighed. "No. She doesn't." He shifted his attention to Eileen. "She's not ready. Not yet."

Eileen looked at the nice man before her and the pretty young woman making her way to the restrooms. "She will be. Probably sooner than you think."

He gave her a half-hearted smile. "I'll be here when she is."

"One word of advice," she said.

Garrett nodded at her.

"Don't wait twenty-five years."

● ● ● ●

As much as Sean wanted to dance with Eileen, he knew that gossip would take over before they had a chance to grow comfortable with the new normal themselves. Instead he slipped his hand under the table and nearly jumped for joy when she held on tight squeezing his.

He'd be a fool if he didn't think someone in the place hadn't noticed him watching her like a lovestruck teen, but they deserved a little privacy so he'd keep up the status quo in public for now.

"That pub is going to be one heck of a hot spot." In the backseat of the quad cab, Finn draped his arm around his beautiful wife. "Should have opened a pub years ago."

"Town wasn't ready for it then." Sean kept both hands on the steering wheel.

"They sure are now," Joanna added.

"It's going to be lots of fun." Eileen looked over her shoulder at the two in the backseat. "And I for one am delighted to have a place to go and unwind after a long day of ranching."

"Well," Sean glanced at her, "you won't have to do that again for a while. Luke will be by tomorrow to load up his cattle and we'll have the fences up again in no time."

"Yep," Finn agreed. "We've got everything secured at Connor's. He and DJ will be over first thing in the morning to pitch in with the fence line."

"Does anyone know how much longer Fancy and her friends will be in town?" Joanna asked.

"Actually, I do." Eileen shifted sideways in her seat for a better view of Joanna and Finn. "Chatted a bit with Allison and they've worked out a plan. Not much different from what she and Ethan had decided. They've been referring to Fancy as Mama Fancy and showing Brittany pictures. They never wanted her to forget who her real mother was. Now that Fancy has turned a corner of sorts, she'll be visiting Tuckers Bluff whenever down time allows."

"But Allison will be more like Brittany's mom than Fancy?"

Sean looked at Eileen and saw the momentary pain in her eyes. "Not more like. Fancy will always be her mom. Allison will just have the job full time."

Joanna sat back looking more confused than when she'd asked, but Sean knew what Eileen meant. The entire relationship would be different because unlike Helen, who could not return to visit her children, Fancy had made choices that in the end were all from a love of her little girl. A little girl she could come back and share time with.

Joanna leaned back against her husband again. "I guess with all the celebrities going home things should return to normal around here."

"Yep," Sean agreed. Everything would be back to normal. Except for one very important thing. Already a great team, he and Eileen were about to get even better.

At the entrance to the ranch, Sean turned the truck onto the property.

"Man," Finn yawned, "I could sleep for a week."

"What is that?" Eileen pointed straight ahead.

The truck headlights bounced up and down the driveway, flashing on dark movement. Sean couldn't quite make out what lie ahead. "Not sure."

As the house drew in closer, the porch light combined with the headlights made their night time visitors easier to see. "Well, I'll be."

Pulling to the side of the house, Sean hopped out of the car first.

Doors slammed behind him.

Before he could reach Eileen's door she was down and out of the truck and moving full speed ahead to the two guests perched, patiently waiting, on the front porch. "What are you two doing here?"

Gray lifted a paw to her and barked. As though agreeing, Mrs. Gray dipped her head and barked too.

Finn laughed. "I should have known." Stopping to pet each dog behind the ears, Finn looped his arm around his wife, and shaking his head, waved goodnight. "Y'all can figure this out. We're hitting the sack."

Down on his haunches, Sean held Gray's head with one hand, scratching under his chin with the other. "Did you know about this all along?"

Gray lifted his head up then down again then, rising to all fours, took a step back. Mrs. Gray came to stand beside him. Both gave a single bark, then tore off around them to the back of the house.

"Think that was a yes?" Sean followed with Eileen on his heels.

The dogs had scurried past the house, around the kennels, and into the barn. In the far corner there were two small mounds of hay neatly arranged. Gray curled up on one and the Mrs. on the other.

"Okay, now I've seen it all." Sean slapped his hat against his leg.

Eileen came up beside him and slid her arm through his. "Do you think this means they'll be staying?"

"I haven't any idea, but they'd be a great asset to the ranch." He turned to look at her. "You know what this means?"

"How foolish of us." Eileen's head tipped back in a short laugh. "Thinking we would get to choose our future."

"These two should have parked their butts here a week ago. Would have saved me a lot of grief."

"Grief?"

His hands rode up the side of her arms. "You know what they say. A person too often doesn't know how much something means to him until he's about to lose it."

"Or has to give it up." Eileen leaned in, pressed her lips to his, then slowly rolled back on her heels.

"Guess this means we're stuck with each other." He smiled.

She grinned back. "Sure does."

Fingers threaded together, they took one last look at the two dogs, all set for the night, a sharp eye on each of their people. The new normal. Two adult dogs for the two adult people. *They should have known.*

MEET CHRIS

USA TODAY Bestselling Author of more than a dozen contemporary novels, including the award winning *Champagne Sisterhood*, Chris Keniston lives in suburban Dallas with her husband, two human children, and two canine children. Though she loves her puppies equally, she admits being especially attached to her German Shepherd rescue. After all, even dogs deserve a happily ever after.

More on Chris and her books can be found at
www.chriskeniston.com

Follow Chris on Facebook at ChrisKenistonAuthor
or on Twitter @ckenistonauthor

Questions? Comments?
I would love to hear from you.
You can reach me at chris@chriskeniston.com

Made in the USA
Coppell, TX
08 February 2023